RICHARD GARCIA MORGAN

The Falls of Mysterion

Tales from Mysterion, Book 2

WAYSTONE
PRESS

First published by Waystone Press in 2017

ISBN: 978-1-7750695-3-9

This book was professionally typeset on Reedsy.
Find out more at reedsy.com

To my wife, Jaime

Join My Readers' Group!

Building a relationship with my readers is one of the best parts of the writing life. I send out occasional newsletters to my Readers' Group with interesting curated content, as well as details of new releases in the Tales of Mysterion and special offers.

And if you sign up to my Readers' Group, I'll send you an excerpt from Book 3, *The Ordeal of Windfire*, FOR FREE.

You can find the link to sign up for my Readers' Group at the end of this novel.

A Note on the Origins of Mysterion

In the beginning, the Wind blew a sphere of space and time as the first light shone out, and the dark chaos yielded to them both. The light itself was so pure that it was invisible, so the Wind opened a window itself and let a portion of chaos in. With all its power, the Wind worked that dark material into earth, air, water, and fire—elements that would catch the light's rays and reflect back its hidden colors. Then, joyfully, it combined the elements in uncountable ways to make the world of Mysterion.

Snow-capped mountains rose toward the sky in the north. Further west and south, the mountains descended to grassy plains, then yielded to swamps, then golden desert sands rolling away in dunes. Further south still, the sands themselves came up against mighty rivers and lush, abundant jungles.

And between the arms of mountains in the north and jungles in the south was the vast ocean of Mysterion, dotted with countless islands all the way to the Edge in the east, where Okean falls...

Having formed the land and the water, the Wind shaped every living creature its imagination could conceive. On the same earth, the worm worked its way through the dark soil while the unicorn frolicked in the sun. In the air, the sparrow darted here and there as the Roc hunted its prey and the Phoenix lived and died in an explosion of fire. In the rivers and streams and beneath the waves of the sea, the jellyfish pulsed among the sea-going dragons diving into the depths.

And so the land and ocean and sky were filled with every fish and bird and animal, for no other reason than that the Wind sought to make the unseen light and its unknowable beauty known.

But what is beauty without someone to see it? So it was that the Wind opened a second time and fashioned another portion of chaos into two races. One was the race of shape-shifters who could take the form of any element they chose. The Wind made them to proclaim the pure beauty of their chosen element.

The Angeli chose air and became the messengers of the Wind's purpose in Mysterion. The mermaids devoted their forms to water, and the Blind Watchmen to earth. Lastly, the Djinn, who were fierce and proud beings, proclaimed fire to be the purest of the elements and superior above all.

And then, finally, the Wind made us, the human race. While the shape-shifters devoted themselves only to a single element, we contained all the elements within ourselves. While the Wind made the shape-shifters to uphold the purity of each element, it made us to sum up all the elements, the whole beauty of Mysterion, and proclaim all that was hidden in the light. Moreover, the Wind called us to preside over the shape-shifters, so that they might not fall into division and conflict over their elements, but might remain united in peace.

However, the Djinn hated the status that the Wind had given them. Why, they demanded, must pure creatures submit to a mixed race? Why should the strongest and fiercest and brightest of the Wind's creatures stand below those in whom the elements had mingled, becoming tainted and corrupt and weak? They swore to subdue all of humanity, and all of Mysterion, under the element of fire.

The Djinn soon learned that they could not force us to submit to this element. However, they learned that we can be limited and enslaved in other ways. We can listen to our hearts over our minds, or our minds over our hearts. We can come to treasure body over soul, or soul over body. We can divide into tribes, preferring our own at the expense of the others. But above all, the Djinn discovered that they could tempt us very easily into preferring our illusions over realities. Thus they learned that if they were clever, they could lead us into forgetting Mysterion as it really is in favor of a world made up of lies and self-deceptions.

So the Djinn came to us in various forms to divide us, from Mysterion, from each other, and from ourselves. Being shape-shifters, they came hidden in the forms of insects, animals, birds, and even human beings, but they found that dreams were their most effective disguise, the most powerful way to control how we think of the world. So they floated into our minds as subtle, pleasant fantasies in which each of us was absolute king or queen over Mysterion, each commanding the rest according to our slightest whim. And when we woke, we found ourselves unhappy, resentful of our responsibilities to care for others and to listen to and follow the Wind that was the true ruler of Mysterion.

That was what led to the first Battle of Mysterion. Those who hated the world as it really is—also called the forgetful ones, or *Lethes*—allied themselves with the Djinn, while the rest—a small remnant—sought the protection of the Angeli. For one hundred days, men and women fought by land and sea, Djinn and Angeli by air, but despite their valor, the People of the Wind were defeated.

The very few remaining scattered in all four directions to live in exile in the outer regions of Mysterion, concealing themselves lest they be found and destroyed. The Angeli, with no one to protect, retreated above the heavens and could do nothing more than keep watch and bear witness as the Lethes and the Djinn overran Mysterion. The Djinn used every growing thing as fuel for their fires, until the land was stripped bare and barren and the waters were brown and grey with loose earth.

The Lethes, finding their world even more hateful than it was before, spent most of their time sleeping, lost in their fantasies. Eventually, they forgot even the existence of their bodies, which shrank into mere husks, and soon ashes covered them over, while the fires of the Djinn continued to burn and the smoke filled the air and storms raged overhead, returning Mysterion to the chaos in which it began.

As their dormant bodies shrank, the spirits of the Lethes escaped and floated down to gather at the base of Mysterion. There they mingled, like an ocean, forming into a single collective dream, a shared illusion in which each of them still claimed to be king or queen alone, only now each had to win his or her claim to power against the others. They even multiplied and passed on their illusions to those who came after them. You may call this shared illusion the "real world," but it is only a part of the real world, fragments mistaken for the whole, parts mistaken for the sum. The Lethes who live in it are truly asleep and waiting to be woken to see the world in all dimensions, as it truly is.

Lethes I

Isabella Morgan ran in the darkness. Overhead the wind whipped the trees around in a frenzy. Far behind her she could still hear her father shouting, "She cut me, the little vixen cut me!" His voice faded as she pressed deeper into the forest. The undergrowth clung to her and the night heat thickened to the consistency of old oil, resisting her. But she struggled on, blind with the tears that rose in sobs.

At last, the trees opened into a small clearing flooded with moonlight. Scattered around the clearing, gravestones, overgrown with moss and lichen and vines, lay in a rough arrangement of rows. Some leaned at odd angles or sank into decay, their inscriptions almost indecipherable. Others stood straight and clean-cut against the assaults of time and decrepitude.

Isabella had discovered the cemetery three years earlier, after a similar incident with her parents. She had come here so many times since that she could find it even when an internal hurricane was tearing her apart, as it was again tonight.

Seized by fits of crying and with her head bowed, she stumbled to her favorite spot at the far corner of the cemetery, where the trees cast impenetrable shadows. The stone there was the largest of the markers, a granite slab worn and rounded with age, grey with lichen, and leaning back slightly. Isabella had cut back the growth around the grave to make room. Now she collapsed against the stone, drawing her knees up to her face and closing her eyes against her tears.

Papa had come home drunk, as always. He and Mama had gone

at each other about the usual suspects: his unemployment, Mama's parentage, and finally—their favorite source of complaint—Isabella. Her boyfriend Maxim was what really set her father off.

Isabella's sobs faded, leaving something dull and empty in their place. This feeling had once disturbed her, but now it came as a relief, almost pleasant. Above, the moon sailed out from behind a cloud. As if disturbed by her recollections, the wind rattled the branches. Clouds drew a curtain over the moon.

Isabella felt a presence nearby. She looked around.

A man appeared in the middle of the cemetery. Isabella could not guess his age. His face could have belonged to any number of people she had met and forgotten. Only the extreme pallor of his complexion struck her as unusual.

Strolling among the stones, he sat down in front of her, cross-legged. She didn't move or draw back. She was used to sitting by the sea road, talking to anyone who happened by. Besides, there was nothing particularly disconcerting about this man, other than a curious deadness in his eyes.

"You look comfortable, Miss," the young man said. "Settling in?" A grin spread over his lips without touching his eyes.

"I like it here," Isabella said.

"Well, at least the dead don't natter your ear off," the man agreed. "I heard a story once of a woman who brought all the news to her husband's grave. Told him about this and that, you know. And what did she get for her troubles? He came back as a poltergeist and tore up her house. Apparently he was upset Rose had sold all his things after he died."

The young man chuckled and shook his head.

"I've heard all the stories," Isabella said. "I don't remember that one."

The young man looked at her, tilting his head. "It happened a long time ago. Long before you were born, when people still believed in poltergeists. No doubt things like that don't happen these days."

"Still," Isabella insisted. "I would know it. I talk to the old-timers."

"Yes." The young man nodded. "I know you do."

Isabella's eyes narrowed. "What do you mean?"

"I've watched you."

She straightened up. "I've never seen you. Who are you, anyway?"

The young man looked mortified. "Did I forget to introduce myself?" He slapped his face. "How terribly rude of me! Well, it's never too late, is it? My name is Malach. Pleased to meet you, Isabella Morgan!"

Isabella regarded the pale, soft-looking hand Malach held out to her.

"I don't know that name," she said.

"Probably not," Malach said. "But you *have* seen me. You just forgot my face. It is rather forgettable, isn't it? Or," he continued, inspired by an afterthought, "perhaps you did not recognize me."

"Why wouldn't I recognize you?" Isabella asked, thinking, *Perhaps he escaped from St. Claire's madhouse.*

Malach shrugged. "Sometimes we are not who we seem. Won't you shake?"

Isabella shook her head. "I don't shake hands with strangers. Especially not in cemeteries at midnight."

"But it's morning already!" Malach cried, gesturing widely at the sky, where the moon had sunk out of sight and the air had lost its impenetrable quality, acquiring a dimension of blue. "And besides, how would you make friends if you did not first shake the hand of a stranger?"

Isabella looked around, surprised at how quickly morning was approaching. "You want to be my friend?"

"Absolutely," Malach declared, stretching his hand further toward her.

"Why?"

"Do friends need a reason to be friends, other than mutual affection?"

"Perhaps I don't want your affection."

Malach raised his eyebrows. "Why not?"

Isabella's smile was twisted. "Are you mad? You're a stranger approaching me in a cemetery!"

Comprehension dawned on Malach's face. "Oh, for goodness' sake, my dear girl... No, no, no! A creature like me does not require such base pleasures! If you only knew... No." He grew serious. "I seek only your welfare. Your freedom, Isabella. Now, come on. Shake, and I will tell all!"

"Fine," Isabella said. "I don't care anyway." Almost carelessly, she reached out. Malach grabbed her hand.

At once, he seemed to explode. His skin darkened. Muscles bulged and coiled in his arms as his suit ripped and vanished. His head stretched into a long, angular shape, like the skull of an ox, while horns spread out above his ears. Wings sprouted from behind his shoulders, reminding Isabella of the illustrations of pterodactyls she had seen in her science textbook.

"Oh, silly me!" he cried, once the transformation was complete. "I seem to have lost my disguise."

Isabella had scrambled around behind the grave marker, her heart throwing itself against her ribcage.

"Surprised?" Malach said.

"What are you?" Isabella shouted.

"Have you ever heard of a genie?"

Isabella said nothing.

"Three wishes? Yes?"

"You... you're a genie?"

"An insult to my kind!" Malach shouted. "No, I am not a genie! I am a Djinn of the tribe of Shaitan!"

"Then why did you disguise yourself?"

"It is necessary to do so for the comfort of weak-minded humans. But in your case, I made an exception."

"Where do you come from?"

"A faraway place. A place you can only imagine." He paused, and then added, "*Can* you imagine such a place? Or is this your idea of paradise?" The air had taken on the translucent quality of early dawn.

The dampness of dew coated Isabella's skin, making her shiver.

"Why are you here?" Malach demanded. "Do you not like your home?"

"No." Isabella's voice shook. "I hate it." She thought, *Three wishes...*

Malach's eyes glowed like coals in the semi-darkness. "Why?"

Her father's feet slapped down the hallway toward her room. He tried the door handle, then pounded.

"Open this door!" he shouted.

"You stay out of here!" she yelled. She was trembling now.

"Didn't I tell you to stay away from Maxim?"

"He's my friend! What do you care?"

"I told you to stay away from him. He's a shady character!"

"It's none of your business!"

"None of my business? I'll give you none of my business. Open this door or I will break it down, I tell you!"

Rummaging in the bureau among her underwear, she found her switchblade and flicked it open. "You don't go crazy," Max had said, when he had entrusted it to her. "But when they come at you, you have to take care of things." He whipped it around as he had seen Bruce Lee do in Fists of Fury.

Isabella spoke at last. "Because my papa is a pig and my mama is a cow."

Malach's eyebrows rose. "Strong words! And what exactly have they done to deserve such condemnation?"

Isabella folded her arms and looked away.

"They get drunk, don't they?"

Isabella looked at him. "If you knew, why did you ask?"

"Because I wanted *you* to tell me," Malach jabbed a claw-like finger at her face. "So they get a little soused! What's so wrong with drowning your sorrows in beer once in a while? After all—"

"That's not all they do."

"Then what?"

Isabella was silent. The memories of the evening were strong upon her.

"Isabella!" her father bellowed.

"Isabella, open the door, baby," her mother bleated. "He's going to kick it!"

"Now you'll see!" her father said. With a loud bang, he kicked at the door. It cracked and shivered but just held. Isabella heard him grunt. He hit again, and the door exploded inward. The way he strode in toward her, with that look on his face, she knew she would be sobbing in the corner when he was done. He wouldn't break anything, but the bruises would last.

"When my father gets drunk—" Tears filled Isabella's eyes, and she stopped. "He hurts me," she managed at last.

Malach's words were laced with a measure of pity. "And your mother?"

Her mother... Mama appeared in the doorway now and saw Isabella pointing the switchblade at her father. She clapped her hands over her mouth and cried, "Oh my Jesus, Pierre and Mary!"

"Stay away from me," Isabella told her father. Then, glancing at her mother, "Both of you, leave me alone!"

"Give that to me." His voice sounded strangled.

"No."

"Give it to me!" He lunged forward. Isabella ducked and stabbed upward. Her father yelled and stumbled sideways, collapsing on her bed. Isabella found herself still holding the knife, dark, sticky blood coating the blade and her hand. Mama rushed forward and collapsed by the bed. "Ray, my love, look what did she did to you!" Then she raised her face to Isabella and spat, "Are you happy now? You killed your own father!"

"She doesn't care," Isabella sniffed. "She just sits there staring in front of her and smoking a cigarette. And when she's sober and I tell her what happened, she looks at me like I'm touched."

"Why don't you run away?"

Isabella looked scornful. "What do you think I'm doing here?"

"But why don't you stay away?"

"Where would I go?" Isabella shouted. "Everyone on this stinking island knows me or my parents! I can't go to Praslin because my papa's family is from there and they'd send me back. I can't go to my auntie—she's such a religious type I couldn't stand her—" As she spoke, Isabella pulled a medallion out from beneath her shirt, sliding it back and forth on its leather cord. It was coin of some sort.

Malach leaned forward with interest.

"I am sorry to interrupt," he said. "But what is that stunning piece of jewelry?"

Isabella paused and looked down at the medallion.

"My papa gave me that," she said. "When I was little. It's a doubloon. He got it from his father, who got it from his father, all the way back. He said our ancestor was hanged as a pirate, and this was part of a great treasure that was lost a long time ago. Our ancestor kept a piece as proof."

"Is that what you talk to the old-timers about?" Malach asked. "To find out clues to the hidden treasure?"

Isabella shrugged.

"Well, I must say, it's a precious gift," Malach murmured. "It reminds me of another I saw once..." He broke off. "A precious gift from someone who cares about you."

"He gave it to me a long time ago," Isabella said. "He was different then."

"So you keep on going back. Because of a single good memory?"

"I said I have nowhere else to go. Besides, it's none of your damn business!"

"But if you could go somewhere else, you would."

"Of course! I'd leave that hole in a heartbeat!"

"Then," Malach said with an arch smile, "why not go somewhere far away, where no one will recognize you?"

"Leave the islands? I can't afford—"

"No, that's not what I mean." Malach paused for emphasis. "I mean go to the place I can show you."

The trees were alive with birds. The sky had paled to the color of roses. The grasses bowed under the dew.

Malach continued, "Imagine a place far away from this suffering. Nobody would know you because no one there remembers this world. They have all forgotten their miserable lives in this hell and found what they were looking for. They are free, you understand? You could get lost and never get found. You could even give yourself a new name." He was looking at her closely now.

Isabella half sniffed, half laughed. Malach grinned and spread his arms. "I don't know—whatever you want!"

"Is that one of the wishes you grant?" Isabella asked. "A new name?"

Malach's grin faded into a cold smile as he shook his head. "I've told you—I don't grant wishes like some fairy-tale creature. I am telling you of Mysterion because I see that you are suffering at the hands of those who should love you. But there is a cost to enter. And that, I'm afraid, is something I cannot waive merely because I happen to like you."

Isabella looked suspicious. "So there is a price."

"Of course," Malach replied. "Everything comes with a price, even friendship—though that is somewhat less tangible than this..." He reached out and opened his hand. Something heavy dropped and dangled at the end of an iron chain. A stone that resembled a piece of charcoal. As she looked, it somehow got blacker and more impenetrable, as if it were feeding on her vision.

"When you take the enchanted stone, you will purchase a Chant that I, the vendor, will pronounce on your behalf, gaining you access to Mysterion forever." Malach's voice had turned dry, like a lawyer reading from a legal document. "In taking the stone, you bind yourself to the condition of purchase, which is service to the Djinn as payment for your entrance. You will serve us until payment is made in full, at which time you will be free to live in Mysterion until your death."

Isabella was silent. She could not believe she was listening to this creature and his insanity of magical stones and imaginary places. And yet here he was before her, holding something truly fascinating.

"How will I," she found herself saying, "how will I serve you?"

"Nothing too onerous," Malach said. "Believe me, you'll be able to do it in your sleep—ha-ha."

Isabella frowned, not understanding the joke. "But what is it?"

"I cannot explain it here. You must come and see in order to understand."

"But supposing I see and I don't want to do it?"

"Then it will be too late, I'm afraid."

Streaks of sunlight now pushed through the trees. She noticed Malach wince and shrink deeper into the shade.

"Don't like the sunlight?" she asked.

"I sunburn easily." Malach's smile was a grimace. "Besides, I cannot be seen in my civvies, so to speak. Which is why I will be leaving in a less than a minute, with or without you."

Isabella shook her head. "I don't know..."

"What do you have to lose? This little cemetery where you come before your time, like little old Rose who couldn't live in reality once she lost her old man? Or perhaps you will miss your parents?"

A wave of indifference swept suddenly over Isabella. Servitude, or this—what did it matter, anyway? Closing her eyes, she reached out and clutched the stone dangling from the Djinn's hand.

Several things happened at once. Malach began to chant in a strange language that seemed to be made only of consonants. Daylight retreated from the cemetery, light sucked back into the east. Darkness rose overhead, and at the same time, with a silent rush, a tide of black water poured out of the trees, flooding the clearing, drowning the graves. It rose up cold around her and swirled around her waist, her chest. Isabella scrambled to her feet, but the black water reached her neck even as she stood up. Malach had vanished in the confusion, and now the freezing water rose over her head. She flailed, tried to pull her way to the surface, but there was no surface to find. Her lungs heaved, and black liquid filled her mouth.

Iron-hard claws dragged her up and out as she coughed up the bitter water. It was night again, and she lay on a patch of white sand in the moonlight. The air stank of pig's excrement.

A voice like nails on a blackboard spoke. "Lift her!"

Upright and hanging from the claws of two creatures who resembled Malach, she looked around her. At the edge of the clearing, a forest reached up like skeletal hands, where a host of Djinn hissed and flapped their wings. Before her stood a bloated, alien-looking baobab tree.

Malach stood beside the Tree. He wore a tattered cloak.

"Welcome to your new home, Isabella Morgan," he said.

He dug his claws into the baobab's trunk and dragged it apart.

"I look forward to observing your suffering. Put her in!"

Her captors dragged her forward. She was hurled into a darkness that stank of sweat and excrement. She hit the ground on her side, and something that felt like ropes enveloped her. Only they weren't ropes... They were more like vines or roots, wrapping themselves around her. She screamed as they worked their way under her skin and into her flesh...

Then, the pain was gone. She found herself lying in her room at home, curled in a fetal position. The night's heat was a solid thing pressing down, with only the space under the door for light. The sharp coir fiber of her mattress mingled with the sweat-stink of a sheet that hadn't been washed since who-knows-when. And her parents' shouting came at her again from under the door.

***

How many times the nightmare repeated itself, she did not know. Over and over it played, like a film clip on a constant loop: her parents shouting, her father's footsteps in the hallway, his pounding on the door. She was on her feet, screaming at him. And then the door came down and her blade did its work.

And then, as if time had broken and reset, she was back on the bed again, hearing them shouting...

After a lifetime, or perhaps it was just a day, the sound of tearing wood interrupted the nightmare. Hard claws dragged her from the cocoon of roots and out onto the sand. Around her, even the dim light was blinding. The world was blurred and distorted, as if she had entered another nightmare.

She rolled onto her side and peered upward. Above her, the Djinn Malach and someone else—an older man with bushy hair—faced each other. Their voices sounded faint and far away, but she could make out their words.

"Is she drained?" the old man was saying.

"Of course she is," Malach said. "We would not have summoned you if she weren't."

"Then I need her restored. She is the one I have been looking for."

"How do you know?" Malach said.

The bushy-haired man looked down at Isabella. She could feel the intensity of his eyes.

"Because I know," he said.

"I am beginning to wonder, Hodoul," Malach said, "if you are more concerned with securing your own legacy than with the task my dearly-departed predecessor, the late Lord Geist, assigned to you."

"I know my purpose," Hodoul said. "I am doing what is required."

"He felt you should not be fed to the Tree," Malach said, as if Hodoul hadn't interrupted. "He allowed you to preserve your memories, so that you could better manage our human harvest. I, on the other hand, am more dubious. I wonder if allowing someone such freedom is wise. It was this kind of naïve trust in humanity that led to Geist's unfortunate demise..."

"I tell you what I told him," Hodoul said. "My position is a dangerous one. I need... I need *alternatives*..."

Malach considered this for a moment.

"I suppose..." he said. "However, you must pay for her restoration."

"With what?" Hodoul said. "You have everything."

"Not everything," Malach said.

Hodoul hesitated. He seemed to be struggling with something.

"Whatever it is," he said finally, "take it. I am a dead man anyway."

Without hesitating, Malach shot out his hand and pushed it into Hodoul's chest. With the other, he reached down and grabbed Isabella's head. As Hodoul moaned and twitched, something bright and pulsing drained from his heart into Malach's claw. At the same time, through his other claw, Isabella felt her consciousness returning. Her hearing and vision sharpened. Now she was awake, though she could not move her limbs. The Tree had sapped her strength.

Malach released her and pulled his claw from Hodoul's chest. Hodoul stumbled back but stayed upright. He took a few deep breaths, then bent and with some gentleness, picked her up.

"You know how to find me," he said to Malach.

"And we will," Malach replied, raising his hand in a mock salute. "Until then, farewell, my dear Jack."

Only as Hodoul started to walk away did Isabella become aware of the crowd of Djinn that surrounded them—a sea of horned skull-like heads and tattered wings, hissing and parting reluctantly to let them pass.

Hodoul looked down at her and smiled. "You will have to get used to them, my dear. They will be your overlords from now on."

Chapter One

Bella Couteau ran in the darkness. The wind roared overhead, keeping pace with her in the trees and muting the slap of her feet on the beaten path. A hundred yards behind came the shouts of her pursuer.

He's definitely falling behind. Not yet, though. She needed to gain at least fifty more yards before she could risk turning off. Slapping at her pocket to make sure her prize was still there, she leaned into her run.

The path angled uphill. The coconut trees retreated. Thicker vegetation closed around her and met overhead, blocking out the sky. The air enclosed her like a damp hand, and fresh rivulets of sweat ran into her eyes. Bella swept a hand over her face and leapt up along the path, trusting instinct and memory to guide her. She could no longer hear him. Now was safe, she decided, and she turned aside, pushing several yards into the bushes before squatting into stillness.

The sound of panting reached her. A light swelled from the direction of the path—Joe Granbousse's lamp—then a gurgling, as if Joe were inhaling water, and his voice, high and petulant:

"Damned—bloody thief—I'll be seeing you marooned with the Blind Watchman by evening. I'll be watching the monster use your guts to clean the flesh from his teeth, by the Tyrant—I'll be laughing..."

Bella grinned to imagine the pear-shaped merchant with the flaps of loose skin under his arms quivering and dripping. For as long as she had been with the Brethren, he had never joined in a raid. This fact alone made him a pleasure to despise. A leech like that could hardly claim the rights of faithful men. He deserved to be stolen from. He practically *begged* for it.

"Yes, sir, absolutely correct sir," came a second voice, breathless and squeaky. Bella chuckled and rolled her eyes. Wherever Joe Granbousse went, Apoojamy was sure to follow, circling like a fruit fly while his head bobbed as if attached to a spring. He was as thin as Joe was fat, reaching as high as the merchant's chest. Apoojamy's limbs jerked and shifted even when he sat, but no matter how slowly his master moved, he always seemed to lag behind.

"We'll both be laughing, sir," Apoojamy continued. "That is an absolute guarantee. I saw the fellow well, sir, quite well. I am almost absolutely one hundred percent certain I could spot the rogue..."

Bella covered her mouth to stop the laughter. Apoojamy had seen her, all right—seen her so clearly he thought she was a *boy*... Well, good! When Apoojamy had descended the stairs into the merchant's cellar and discovered her crawling back up the hatchway whose lock she had picked, he started shouting, "Stop thief! Stop, despicable delinquent!" and then, calling up the stairs to the merchant, "Come, sir, come!" She had not known until now whether he had identified the shape of her body.

Clearly not, the arse-kisser.

"Let them be lined up," he was squeaking. "And I shall certainly identify him, almost absolutely I shall."

"And well you may, Apoojamy," Joe Granbousse replied. "Well you may. For I will not be letting this rest, of that you can be assured, Apoojamy. It was two pounds of my best Dragon's claw powder! Do you realize the labor of acquiring such a quantity? Not to be taken lightly."

"No indeed, sir," Apoojamy replied. "I would never dream of making light. I above all know..."

"Then you'll know that I will not be taking this lightly, Apoojamy."

"Almost certainly, sir."

"There is a Code, Apoojamy, outside of which is darkness and anarchy, without which enterprising men are unable to earn their keep, put bread on the table, and store up against the day!"

"A most honorable Code, sir," affirmed Apoojamy. "Praise the king!"

"Praise him indeed," Joe Granbousse said absently. "And this Code, as I said, has today been violated!"

"Most viciously, sir."

"And I will be recompensed!"

"Yes, yes, yes!"

Bella suppressed a sigh. *When will these idiots shut up? I need a hit.*

"Now, Apoojamy," Joe Granbousse continued. "Let us be clear."

"Crystal, sir."

"You say that you spotted this fiend."

"Almost certainly, sir," Apoojamy declared.

"*Almost* certainly?" Joe Granbousse repeated.

"I am begging your pardon, sir..."

"Did you *almost* see him, or did you *certainly* see him?"

"Absolutely, sir. He was short and thin, like a stray cat, and his hair was tangled..."

There was a silence. "Is that all?"

"He wore pantaloons and a linen shirt..."

"By the Wind, Apoojamy!" Joe Granbousse roared. "You're describing half the boys and men in the Camp!"

Apoojamy whimpered.

"I know his shape, sir," Apoojamy whined. "I can exactly certainly spot the bugger. Of this I am certain..."

"Fine," Joe cut in. "Let us go on a little further now, in case we scent smoke and locate the criminal. If so, we will execute justice. If not, we shall bring the matter before the king in the morning."

"A most excellent declaration, sir!" cried Apoojamy.

Joe Granbousse's sigh was audible.

"I swear, Apoojamy," he said. "You have your head so far up my backside that sometimes I don't know my end from your beginning. Now, onward. I am tired, and honest men need their rest."

The glow of the lamp faded as the two men walked on up the

path. Rather than rising, however, Bella shifted herself into a more comfortable position and waited. Several minutes later, the light reappeared and floated back toward the flatland. The men were in full flow again.

". . . and so I said to him, I said, 'This is the finest stock west of the Tyrant's lands.' 'Then why,' he says, 'does it taste like paraffin?' He doesn't believe me, I can tell that now. So I say something about the cane and the soil in which it lies, and how sometimes this can add new flavors..."

"Indeed I remember it, sir," Apoojamy declared. "It was a most ingenious solution to your dilemma!"

"Then you will also remember that he didn't swallow that load!" Joe Granbousse snapped. "You will remember how he started threatening me! So I offered him a discount on the next flagon..."

"And he accepted! The same stuff, too! Yes, yes. I perfectly remember. How utterly commendable..."

Their voices faded. Bella pushed her way out of the bushes and stood with her head tilted. Sifting through the din of the crickets to the moan of the onshore wind further on and the almost imperceptible hiss-and-suck of the waves over the sand, she could hear nothing that suggested the whining of petulant merchants and their squeaking assistants. She stretched herself, yawned, and ambled back down the path. Reaching the flats, she wound her way among the coconut trees until they fell behind and her feet sank into the powdery sand. Full in her face now, the wind was a single breath exhaled from the east. The open ocean heaved and hissed in and out over the sand, while the moon shattered into fragments over its surface.

Bella barely glanced at the sight—she was thinking about something else and looking around for a place to light up. A large rock lay nearby, just above the line of seaweed. Bella made her way toward it as quickly as the clinging sand allowed. Relieved, she lowered herself down against the cool stone. She would stay dry when high tide came, unseen from the head of the beach.

At last, her hands shaking, she scrabbled in the pocket of her pantaloons and pulled out the item she had stolen from Joe Granbousse's storehouse—an oilskin pouch tied with laces. Opening it in her lap, she carefully reached into the sleeve and fingered the coarse grains of Dragon's claw, then bent to inhale its biting odor on her fingertips. From her other pocket she pulled a small clay pipe with a silver lid clasped over the bowl. Quick with desperation, she filled the pot with the Dragon's claw, then pulled out a box of matches. She swore as the wind killed both the first and second attempts inside her cupped hands, before the contents of the bowl caught and hissed. Bella snapped the lid closed and sucked deeply at the pipe. The smoke raked at her lungs, and she shuddered. The pain took longer to fade than when she first used Claw, but fade it did, giving way to the numbness she had been craving. Bella exhaled as she sank back against the rock, feeling her whole body dissolve into its surface.

Perhaps I will sleep tonight, she thought. Not that she cared much either way. This would not be the first sleepless night of her life. For as long as she could remember, she had suffered from insomnia. Even among those faint outlines of her life before Mysterion, before she emerged from the Tree, she could remember sitting awake in a dark place while two people shouted at one another somewhere nearby.

Couteau was the name she had given herself when she came to the Brethren, because she liked the sound of it. *A pirate should have a sharp name*, she thought, staring up at the stars that traced infinite spirals and trails across the black sky. Bella the Knife, that was sharp. She had proved it, too, on countless occasions. *Bella Couteau—touch me and I'll cut you.*

When she had come out of the Tree, all that remained in place of her heart and mind had been a dull cloud. She could think with a greater clarity than ever before, and yet nothing had any substance. Things and people, and even her own thoughts and feelings and actions, drifted over to her from across the span of a vast abyss. So, whether she slept or not any more, it didn't seem to matter. Every moment had become little more than a kind of sleepwalking.

Bella drew deeply on the Claw pipe. The stars had faded. The wind on her face was cool, tinged with the early morning. The tide had peaked. Spray touched her legs as the waves broke close by, but she made no attempt to pull in. The Claw was working its magic—her eyelids drooped. Then, just before she fell into oblivion, desolation swept in from the wings of her heart. The urge to cry out welled up in her throat, became unbearable, and receded.

Darkness came over Bella Couteau.

Chapter Two

She woke to a pinch on her hand. She dragged her eyelids open. A hermit crab had her thumb gripped in one claw. Irritated, Bella swung the crab against the rock behind her with a sharp *crack*. It released its grip and lay with legs kicking at the sky. Bella stood and dusted sand from her pantaloons. She looked over the water. The sea was a red mirror, the sun not yet breaking the horizon. Somewhere over there was the Tyrant's land. *The Tyrant and his slaves*, she thought.

But she could not sum up her usual contempt, either for the Wind People or for their tyrant Elder. Instead—she couldn't believe herself—she found herself curious. What would it be like to live as one of *them?* She shoved the thought away. *What's the matter with you, Couteau?* She retrieved her Claw pipe from where it had fallen and noticed the crab still wriggling on its back.

"Stupid creature," she muttered. Placing her heel in the middle of the crab's body, she ground it into the rock. There was something reassuring about the way it cracked and squirted under her foot.

She turned away from the sea, where the sun was now rising, and strode to the head of the beach and into the trees. She intersected the path from the night before and ran along it through the forest. The air, though humid, was still cool from the night. Once her stiffened muscles had eased, she moved quickly, her body refreshed by sleep and her head only slightly foggy from the Claw.

The trees thinned and gave way to scrub. The path wound among granite boulders. Bella slowed only on the steepest parts, until she reached the pass that crossed to the western side of the island. Ahead, the path dropped away in sharp angles to where the forest began, and fingers of smoke and a pall of grey haze over the trees betrayed the presence of Hodoul's Camp. Beyond lay the circle of Hodoul's Bay, its green water enclosed on two sides by sheer granite cliffs. The cliffs curved together to a narrow mouth, where cannon emplacements bristled like the teeth of a barracuda, ready to welcome visitors from rival Brethren crews. From her height, Bella saw the sentries slumped back against the barrels—asleep.

Within this naturally fortified harbor floated the ships under the command of His Highness, Jack Hodoul. As the leader of the Brethren Alliance, he commanded the largest fleet. The other four Princes combined could not equal this assembly of scimitar-shaped dhows, squat square-riggers, corsairs, and sleek schooners—all their spars bare as they rocked and swung on their anchors.

Their decks were deserted, and Bella frowned. *All the sentries sleeping!* she thought. *Leaving us exposed—slack dogs! I should report them for a whipping.* She wouldn't do it, of course. Some things might not be written in the Code, but they were just as sacrosanct. *Besides, he probably knows anyway.* No one had put anything over on Hodoul yet, at least not as far as she could remember. Some of the Brethren even believed he had bewitched houseflies to serve as his spies.

He's watching, she reassured herself. *One way or the other, he's watching.*

Leaping from rock to rock, she followed the path down to the Camp. Just beyond the tree line stood a fence. Thorns and vines, planted side by side years ago, had grown and intertwined into a solid wall that sealed off the Camp's western border. She wondered if this sentry was also asleep. She had slipped through easily enough last night, but daylight was a different matter. If they caught and searched her, she would lose the whole stash of Claw.

Angling off the path, she approached the arched wooden gate with the stealth of a wild creature. As usual, the carved doors stood open to allow early traffic with the surrounding camps. Only one sentry stood guard in front of the gate with a fire-rifle—an immense black man who resembled the overflow of an underground volcano. He wore nothing but a pair of maroon leggings and a bronze band on his upper right arm. His cannonball head gleamed in the sun.

Seeing him, Bella knew why the king had assigned him to guard alone—Disagree was worth twenty of the rest.

With a rare rush of affection, she abandoned all her precautions, pushed through the undergrowth, and burst out onto the path at a full run. The sentry, startled, brought up his musket. Then he saw Bella, and his round face cracked into a wide grin before regaining its customary composure. He lowered the gun and stood waiting.

She stopped a few feet from him.

"Hello, Dis," she said.

Dis regarded her for a moment, then shook his head.

"Dis is not my name," he rumbled.

Bella threw up her hands.

"Well, what kind of name is 'Disagree,' anyway?" she cried.

"The one my Mama give me," he replied.

"But it's not a name. It's something you do."

"It's a name."

"No. Smith is a name. Pillay is a name. Disagree is a verb, as in, I *disagree* with you on that point!"

"It's a name," Disagree insisted. "It's aristocrat."

"Here we go again," Bella said, rolling her eyes.

"It is," Disagree said. "I only remember one thing about the lower world. I was a slave, and my master is called something like 'Disagree.' Then the one of the Overlords come and free me from my chains..."

"No one remembers their time before the Tree. You made your name up, just like the rest of us."

"I have no reason to do that."

"Yes you do—to be contrary."

Disagree grinned. "I disagree. You remember your name, Miss Mor—"

"All right, all right," Bella interrupted, raising her hands. "Leave that alone. Hello, then, Monsieur *Disagree*!"

"Hello, then, Miss *Couteau*," Disagree said with a smile.

They made their way to the side of the gateway, its frame posts carved with tangled snakes. Each of the gates depicted the semblances of two Djinn—massive horned figures encircled with the swirling lines of chaos. Bella and Disagree sat down against the arched posts.

"So?" Disagree asked, after a short silence.

"So what?" Bella poked at the black earth with her feet.

"You get what you want?"

Bella shrugged.

"They see you?" Disagree asked.

"Apoojamy came down as I was leaving."

"Oh."

"He didn't see me, though."

"How do you know?"

"I heard them talking," Bella said. "He thought I was a boy."

"Oh," Disagree said. "Well, good, then."

"Yes," Bella replied, meeting his eyes for the first time. "It was good."

Disagree did not flinch from her look.

"Probably not over yet, though," he warned.

"So?" Bella said. "I'll deal with that too, if I have to."

"You say it," Disagree said, looking away into the distance.

"Damned right," Bella said. "And there's no need to lecture me about it either!"

"All I say is I know the king, that's all."

"So what?"

"He knows you leave last night. Guaranteed."

Her stomach tightened in fear.

"I doubt it," she declared. "I'm too good for that."

"You think?" Disagree murmured, raising his eyebrows.

"And—" Bella hesitated. "So what if he knows? If he summons me,

I'll come, that's all. I take an equal share, just like the others, and I'll stand on my own feet and answer for myself."

"You know," Disagree said, "He write that Code…"

"I know that, Dis!" Bella flared.

"All right," Disagree said. "I'm just saying…"

"I know what you're saying, and I understand!" Her voice was higher now.

"All right, then," Disagree muttered, lowering his eyes. After a moment, Bella looked away through the trees.

"Why do you always have to get so worked up?" she said at last.

"I just think of you, Bella."

"You think too much," Bella said, and then she glared at him. "Papa!"

"Huh!" Disagree sniffed. "If you are my daughter…"

"Yes, yes, I know," Bella laughed. "You'd make me a respectable pirate!"

"Better than wander around in darkness doing who knows what."

"I am not your daughter, Dis," Bella said quietly. "I'm your friend."

"Yes." Disagree nodded. "We are friends."

"So try not to worry like a papa, all right? I had that already."

"All right," he muttered. "Sorry."

"That's all right—my friend." Bella reached out and covered Disagree's hand with her own. They sat in silence for several minutes. Morning sunlight now fell in bright, dusty bars through the forest. Go-away birds shrieked and squabbled among the golden apple trees. The cool of dawn was retreating before the hot bath of day. From the forest behind her, mongrels barked, and a shrill voice berated someone. The sounds evoked a trace of last night's sadness. She began fiddling with the medallion around her neck. It was a single doubloon hung from a leather cord. Along with her switchblade, it was her only possession from before the Tree. She fingered the coin, wondering how many hands had caressed it before her.

"Dis?" she said at last.

"Yes, Bella."

Bella turned the coin between her fingers, loving the buttery smoothness of the ancient gold. "Have you ever gotten the feeling that you were someone else and you were watching yourself do things?"

"How do you mean?" Disagree frowned.

"Like you were inside someone else's head or something."

Disagree considered. "Not really. I always see with my own eyes."

Bella smiled. "That's for certain." She dropped the medallion back into her shirt and chewed her nail.

"What's wrong, Bella?" Disagree asked. "Are you all right?"

Bella dropped her hand into her lap. "Fine," she said. "I'm hungry, that's all."

"I bring some breakfast with me," Disagree said, gesturing to a cloth-wrapped bundle tucked against the foot of the gatepost behind them. "I bring enough for you too."

Bella grinned. "Of course you did."

They ate fried plantains, dried mackerel, and fresh coconut milk straight from nuts that Bella picked in a nearby tree. They had almost finished when they heard Herald Bouteille calling in the distance behind them. "Attend! Attend! The king seeks challengers!" he intoned. "Attend! Attend! The king seeks a worthy challenger!"

Disagree and Bella stared at one another. Bella wiped her mouth and breathed out. The last time the king had called for challengers, the winner had gone on to captain his own ship, with his own crew... She shivered. This was the opportunity she had been hoping for.

Disagree broke into her thoughts as if he had overhead her.

"Perhaps it is not what you think," he warned. "Perhaps it turns out not as you hope."

"I don't care," Bella replied, leaping to her feet and dusting herself off.

"What do you challenge?" Disagree said without getting up.

"For me to know," she said, starting up the path.

"You are sure, Bella?"

Bella threw up her hands without looking back. "Enough! I'm sure, all right?"

"All right," Disagree muttered.

"You want to come and hear it?" Bella looked back at him.

Disagree shook his head. "I do enough over here. With the birds and the coconuts falling, I'm busy enough."

Bella laughed and raised her hand. "Bye then, Monsieur Disagree!"

"Goodbye, Miss Couteau," he replied. But Bella was already running up the path to the parlay square.

Chapter Three

The morning heat slowed Bella to a fast walk as she hurried along the path. The first houses appeared among the trees—wooden shacks on stilts. Torn mosquito netting and shutters covered their windows. Thatched roofs sagged and rotted in patches, like the fur of a mangy animal. The space around each house was a chaos of overturned barrels, broken furniture, and garbage, over which emaciated mongrels fought. Mosquitoes and flies formed a permanent cloud overhead.

Brethren emerged from the squalor as Bella passed, flowing together onto the path. There were men of every shape and color, but their unshaven faces, unwashed clothes, and stench had reduced them to a single homogeneous mob. Their eyes contained the same dullness induced by addiction to Claw. Some of them nodded at her and one another, but most fixed their eyes on the distance, jostling and pushing to get ahead, each of them lost in a single-minded purpose.

Most of the women wore dresses that dirt had rendered an identical grey. Although they walked together, discussing the king's call for a challenge, Bella knew from experience their camaraderie was an illusion. *Make no friends and keep your enemies within reach*—the older shrews had taught her this lesson soon after she arrived. So she walked by herself, not looking at or talking to them as she strode past. Her aloofness drew a shrill commentary:

"It takes a little more than pants to be one of the boys, dearie!"

"And you'll never have it. No matter how hard you try!"

A shriek of laughter rose up at the joke. Bella's face did not change, but her hand dropped into her pocket.

"Perhaps it's because she hasn't got much on offer," a young one giggled.

"Well," came a reply, "she may get a taker anyway. Some of them like the girlie boys, if you catch me."

More laughter. Without a word, Bella whipped her hand out of her pocket and turned on the latest speaker, flicking out her switchblade. The woman screamed and reached into the folds of her dress, but before she could find her own blade, Bella was on her. A whispering, tearing sound of cloth, and the victim stood naked, clutching the shreds of her clothing about her. Bella leapt at her next tormentor, slitting the dress off her back before she could run more than a few paces. She caught and stripped a third before she reached her house and the last at her front door. Then she folded and pocketed the blade, and strode off along the path in silence, leaving her victims naked and cowering in a circle of jeering spectators.

A few minutes later, she arrived at the parlay square—a smooth patch of sand, twenty yards on each side. To the right, the breakers rolled in from the mouth of the bay and exploded on the sand. Lining the other three sides of the square and facing the coolest breezes off the sea were the houses of the most prominent Brethren families, whose bloodlines led back to the very beginning. Unlike the houses deeper in the forest, these buildings were clean, with wide verandas and roofs of wood tiles. Some even had sentries posted at their front steps.

At the far end of the square, shielded by a grove of lime trees, was the house of the king himself. Bella had never been there. Soon after she arrived, she had heard stories of Brethren who had approached too close, uninvited, only to disappear. One night, she had woken to the sound of screaming. Bella shuddered and focused her attention on the center of the square.

The parlay platform stood on pylons and, above it, the skull and crossbones fluttered and flashed in the sun. Herald Bouteille waited there, tall, angular, and impatient, rocking from side to side as the

Brethren flowed out of the forest and gathered into a jostling pool around the platform.

Bella eased her way through the crowd toward the platform. She did not jostle too hard, in case she provoked a fight. In spite of her care she drew a few growls at her passing, but she continued to work her way in until she reached a spot three yards from the platform where the crowd grew too dense. Push further and she would get a knife between the ribs.

Herald Bouteille strutted in tight circles on the platform, hands still on his hips. He resembled a rooster about to announce the dawn. As the stream of Brethren from the forest finally slowed to a trickle and stopped, the Herald turned to face his audience. He lifted his chin, and silence descended.

"Brethren, I call ye to strength unbound!" he cried in a guttural bass. It was the customary formula for a challenge, and a cheer went up from the crowd. "Who shall prevail? Who shall be cunning? The one who pities not, or else feeds the worms! The king will know this steadfast man," Herald Bouteille continued. "He rewards him who will not bend! Who will triumph, who'll meet his end?" Herald Bouteille slapped his thigh to the end-rhyme. More loud cheering, which died swiftly into an expectant hush. Bella shivered. Now he would announce it.

"His Highness King Hodoul calls for a Brother to take a claw from Leviathan *without* breaking the Charter."

A second passed while these words sank into Bella's mind. A second, while she registered it, made the connection, and realized that the single greatest stroke of luck of her life had descended. She knew beyond all uncertainty that she alone could win this challenge. Her discreet inquiries had assured her that the secret she had been keeping now for several weeks, hoping for an opportunity to use what she knew, was hers and hers alone.

It's finally here, she thought. Blood roared in her ears.

"It's madness!" cried Guillotine, a scarred, balding man who had grown and tied the remnants of his hair into a pigtail. His cry unleashed a storm of protest that broke against the platform in waves. The Herald was unperturbed by the threats on his life, the aspersions cast against his parentage, the calls to open rebellion against a king who no longer deserved the loyalty of his Brethren. He simply waited until they lost impetus, then raised his hand. The crowd fell into an uneasy, sullen silence, and Herald Bouteille regarded them calmly.

"The king is aware of the dangers," he said. More muttering, and he raised his voice. "But he believes that there is at least one from his crew who is worthy and able to take it!" Then, Bella saw the Herald's eyes come to rest on her. A prickle ran up her spine, igniting her face with fire.

"No one's crazy enough to—" someone began. Then Bella raised her hand.

"Couteau," the Herald said. She was sure she could hear his relief in his voice.

She took a deep breath.

"I take the challenge," she said in a loud, clear voice.

In the hush that followed, Bella could hear the roar of waves on the beach and the steady *thwup, thwup* of the flag above them. She looked straight ahead at Herald Bouteille, keeping him out of focus so that she could not see his exact expression. But she could feel the eyes of the Brethren on her. They were not friendly eyes. *Any moment now*, she thought.

"Bold little strumpet!" a woman shrieked. "Thinks she can come to an adult gathering and play us for fools—!"

"I have a right, like anyone else," Bella said, wondering if they could hear her voice quiver.

"This is a *challenge*!" a tall, sallow-faced man beside her replied. His spittle flecked her cheeks as he leaned toward her. "This is serious business concerning the king, not the fantasy of some fifteen-year-old twit who thinks she has inherited the powers of a Djinn!"

Bella turned and met his eyes, trying not to flinch.

"This is not a fantasy," she said. "I can do it. Can you?"

"I don't waste my time with madness!" the man cried.

"Get lost, Couteau!" someone called. "You're wasting our time!"

"Go dig a hole and bury yourself!"

"Jump off a cliff!"

"That's enough!" Herald Bouteille cut in. The noise subsided.

"Come forth, Sister Bella," said the Herald. With her heart stumbling, Bella strode forward, ignoring the glares and muttering as the Brethren parted for her. She reached the platform, hoisted herself up, and planted herself beside the Herald, her chin raised.

"You know how to say it?" the herald asked Bella in a low voice.

"Yes," she replied. Taking a deep breath to slow her beating heart, she cried, "On my honor, I take the king's challenge to get a claw from the Leviathan..." she paused. "Or die in the trying!"

"Our Sister has challenged," the Herald said. "Will anyone else?"

A silence followed, punctuated by whispering. Then Guillotine grinned, exposing a row of gold teeth.

"Time to slap the upstart down," he growled. "I'll do it."

A ragged chorus of agreement.

"You also accept the challenge?" Herald Bouteille asked, throwing a nervous glance toward the king's house. "It is not in the proper order..."

"You can shove your proper order where no one would want to look," Guillotine replied. "Yes, I accept."

Herald Bouteille's voice rose above the cheers. "Very well! Call out the boats! To the North Point deep!"

Chapter Four

Of all the seagoing dragons in Mysterion, Leviathan had survived the longest. Before the rise of Hodoul, the pirate gangs had hunted and killed dragons for their claws in the western seas all the way up to the edge of the Blind Watchmen's territory, beyond which they dared not venture.

Eventually the dragons had withdrawn, their natural friendliness betrayed too often by the harpoons and cannons of the hunting parties. They had become so rare and difficult to find that only a few had the skill and patience to hunt them. These had formed a crew known as the Claw-Men, and they devoted themselves to hunting dragons and selling Claw powder to anyone who could pay. Before the Treaties were signed, they were the most powerful among the countless rival crews that feuded among the western islands. The Claw-Men delighted in pitting their customers against each other and watching them splinter into smaller and smaller factions, using their bloody feuds to raise their prices and enrich their profits.

Then Hodoul had descended on them from the Overlords' island, claiming to be their emissary, the bringer of order and justice. Using cunning and diplomacy whenever he could, and ruthlessness when he had to, he had united the factions in a single great crew against the Claw-Men. At last, he launched all his ships, besieged the hunters' island, and in a single day wiped them from existence. He kept only one of his enemies alive—an old hunter named Zarastra—just long enough to guide him on one more dragon hunt before cutting his throat.

That was how Hodoul caught Leviathan. But instead of killing the beast and taking his magnificent, five-foot-long claws as a prize, he bound and dragged Leviathan back to his island, where he leashed him to the northern cliffs on a two-hundred-yard-long, six-inch-thick chain. At that point, the island dropped into an underwater sinkhole, which formed a perfect run for Leviathan. Then Hodoul wrote a Charter protecting him and any other dragon from hunting, on pain of death.

It was said Hodoul signed the Charter with his own blood. And yet the Claw powder had continued to circulate. Everyone knew that Joe Granbousse had a full store and a monopoly on the drug. The merchant had set the price low enough to keep Claw within reach, but high enough to keep it scarce and everyone desperate. The king turned a blind eye to his inflation in exchange (some suspected) for a share of the profits—though no one would dare say so out loud.

Even the Princes—who had broken away from Hodoul after the defeat of the Claw-men—sent emissaries every year to negotiate a supply of Claw from Granbousse and satisfy their own crews' need. The most astute among the Brethren wondered at times if the king's hold over the Princes, and their grudging submission to his rule, had less to do with honoring the Treaties than with their fear that Hodoul could at any time cut off their only supply of Claw once and for all.

But the real question was, how did they get a steady supply of claws from only one dragon? Isabella was certain some of the older Brethren must have known; they had been present for that legendary hunt. But they weren't talking, perhaps afraid that if they, someone might find out and turn off the supply of the magic powder that lifted them to the heights—for a time at least.

***

The flotilla of ships inched up toward North Point, their sails flashing and their hulls heeled far over in the gale that roared around the headland, whipping foam off the green surface. Bella stood in the bow of the king's own sloop, *La Justice*. The jagged cliffs towered three hundred feet above her. Bella saw none of it. She had retreated into the mist of her memory.

Moments before they weighed anchor, the king and his guards had emerged from the royal house, marched down to a skiff on the beach, and skimmed out to the sloop. As the king stepped on board, Bella had knelt with the rest of the crew, waiting to see if he would approach her. But other than a nod at the general obeisance and a word acknowledging the Herald's murmured greeting, the king had allowed himself to be escorted below without a glance in her direction.

Following a respectful pace behind the king had been Joe Granbousse and Apoojamy. This in itself was not unusual, as the king frequently sought the merchant's counsel. Today, however, Apoojamy had kept glancing in her direction. As the retinue crossed the deck, she had met his eyes. His eyes widened, and she looked away. Then Joe had glanced backward, frowned, and muttered something. Apoojamy, realizing he had fallen more than two steps behind his master, scurried forward, and they disappeared down the steps to the stateroom. The crew returned to its tasks.

As the challenger, Bella had received the honor of commanding the king's ship, which exempted her from her usual duties. She paced the deck in circles, chewing on her fingernail as her thoughts tumbled.

He recognized me! No, not possible. It was too dark. He couldn't possibly have seen your face, just relax.

To distract herself, she looked around for her opponent's ship. Twenty yards to starboard, a large dhow whose Arabic name meant *Tongue of the Devil* heeled away on the port tack. The squat shape of Guillotine pressed against the windward railing. He was staring out toward the two-hundred-yard-perimeter where the green water spun in all directions, kicked into madness by the confluence of two currents. That was the pit, but no sign of Leviathan yet.

Poor Guillotine, she thought with a grin. *He's probably wondering what the hell he's let himself in for.*

She felt sorry for him—not sorry enough, though, to tell him her secret. One night, several months earlier, Bella had escaped the camp without being seen and crept up an overgrown path to the edge of the forbidden northern cliffs above Leviathan's run. She spent the nights that followed there, huddled under a scraggly lime tree, enjoying the wind that blew full in her face along with an uninterrupted view of the moonlit ocean and flickering lights from the islands where the Princes had their camps. She stayed away from the edge of the cliff because of her fear of heights—until one sleepless night, when curiosity and boredom got the better of her.

Below, in the wild dark waters of his run, Leviathan circled and dove, his chain whipping back and forth. Turning onto his back, the dragon pedaled the air, like a dog scratching itself on the grass. Looking at those legs, Bella had wondered at the immense curved claws that glinted in the moonlight. She wondered how big a bag she would need to carry the Claw they would produce. She would be richer than Joe Granbousse, perhaps as rich as the king...

At that moment, the dragon roared and leaped several feet in the air, all that his stubby wings would allow. He rushed at the cliff with a wake of phosphorescent water spreading behind him. Thinking he had seen her and forgetting he was chained, Bella leapt back. But Leviathan did not reach up to clamber up the cliff face. Instead, he swam directly into the cliff and disappeared. From her angle, she could not see where the entrance was. She assumed it was one of those cracks that split the rock face and ran deep into the island, wide at the bottom and narrowing rapidly as it went up until it vanished, making access impossible from above.

Leviathan did not emerge again that night. Two nights later, however, she returned to spy on him and noticed that his claws had been cut down to the nub. Within two weeks, they reached the same length as before—almost five feet from root to tip. Then they shrank again, only to reappear seven days later. Only after the third time did Bella finally understand what was happening to his claws, and the realization gripped her with excitement. All she needed then was a way to reach Leviathan's cave, if only for five minutes. She'd be rich.

She had dreamed about it for days, imagining how she would do it but always coming up short against the Charter and what would happen if she dared even to approach the dragon's run in a boat. And then came beautiful Herald Bouteille, with his cockerel strut and his "impossible" challenge, looking at her with the eyes of her destiny. Not to mention good old Guillotine, stepping into his doom right when he needed to. The best versions of her plan had called for a distraction, but nothing in her wildest imaginings came close to *this.*

Bella shivered now in the gale, nibbling her nails. *And if anyone's smart enough to survive, Guillotine is.*

She followed Guillotine's gaze back toward the dragon's run. The Brethren's motley assortment of ships had roughly lined the perimeter of the two-hundred-yard mark. Bucking and tossing against the wind and the south-running current, they struggled to maintain position under shortened canvas. Bella examined her own position. The helm had followed her instructions, not allowing the other ships to get between them and the cliff. Still, they were not close enough—fifty yards or more from where the glass-green waves slid up to shatter against the sheer rock.

She turned and ran aft along the railing to where the helm, a short, slant-eyed man with hair and a goatee like black flames, stood with his feet braced apart against the weight of the wheel. He nodded inscrutably at Bella as she reached him, then turned his eyes back to the sea. Ah-Time was always the professional. Today, however, he would have to take a few risks.

"I need to be closer!" Bella said, steadying herself against the wheel housing. "No more than fifteen yards!"

Ah-Time shook his head.

"Too crazy," he said. "This is safe."

"I have the right!" Bella shouted. "It's my challenge!"

"It's my helm," Ah-Time replied, his face expressionless. "My responsibility."

Bella clenched her jaw.

"Then I relieve you!" she declared.

"You have your way," Ah-Time said, and dropped his hands from the spokes. Instantly, the wheel spun out of control, the deck canting as the ship bore away from the wind. Taken off guard, Bella dove forward. A wheel-handle slammed into her shoulder and she screamed, falling to her knees. A moment later, the pressure eased, and she looked up. Disagree held the wheel with one hand. With the other, he reached down and raised her to her feet.

"You didn't need to do that," Bella said, massaging her bruised shoulder.

"You supposed to get yourself killed," Disagree replied. "Not turn yourself into a wheel-stop."

Herald Bouteille appeared at the top of the steps and called, "His Majesty asks that you not treat his ship so roughly. He says that he was gracious enough to lend it to you for this purpose, but he would like it back in one piece if at all possible!"

Some of the crew laughed at this, and Bella felt her face getting hot.

"Inform His Majesty that the deed will be done without harm to his ship!" she shouted at Bouteille. The Herald raised his eyebrows in disbelief, inclined his head, and disappeared below.

"And you dogs can just get back to work!" she said to the crew before turning on Disagree with a scowl.

"You're supposed to be in the rigging," she hissed. "Not playing Daddy again and embarrassing me!"

Disagree shrugged.

"No one else can get you out," he said. "Least of all you." And before Bella could open her mouth to answer back, he added, "You go back to your craziness. I make sure you are close enough."

Bella glowered at him a moment, then turned on her heels and strode to the railing where a coil of rope lay and, on top of it, a large grappling hook. Bella knotted a hangman's noose around one of the cleats and then hefted the hook, swinging it a few times around her head before allowing it to drop to her side. When she was ready, she looked back at Disagree.

"Bear off," she called. "But don't *look* as if you're bearing off. I don't want Guillotine guessing anything."

Her opponent's ship was moving in the precise opposite direction of their own, bearing off on the port tack so that it lay broadside to the semicircle of wild water that was the dragon's run. Bella could see Guillotine gesticulating by the rail as several crewmembers hefted a skiff over the side. It hung there, ready to be lowered into the water, while Guillotine loaded a bundle almost as long as he was. *A net*, Bella thought, filled with admiration. *Good thinking.*

He might even stand a chance, with a net.

"This is it," Disagree called to her. "No closer."

Bella looked. Thirteen yards from the railing, the open sea broke against the cliff at a line of rocks encrusted with barnacles and seaweed. One of these boulders looked to her as if it might hold the hook quite nicely. From there, she could scale the cliff to the cave entrance.

"Hold," she ordered.

Disagree spun the wheel, and the sloop turned slightly into the wind, spilling her sails, slowing until she was locked "in irons."

Guillotine was climbing into the skiff now. He was readying the oars, waving a signal. With the crewmen working the ropes, the skiff dropped to the water in a white explosion. At once, Guillotine cast off, manned the oars, and pulled away from the dhow into the dragon's run.

Bella lifted the hook and whirled it several times above her head before letting fly. The hook landed with a clatter against the outcropping, then slid off into the water. Cursing, Bella pulled it in. As the grappling iron rose to the railing, dripping, she heard shouting behind her.

"The beast!"

"*Le monstre!*"

Bella turned to see Leviathan break the surface in a mushroom cloud of foam. An acrid whiff of sulfur and dead fish came to Bella, even from this distance. The dragon's head was the size of a full-grown horse and seemed to have been welded from cast-iron scrap. Sharp wing-shaped edges adorned the smoking nostrils. Opening his mouth, he revealed rows of spiny teeth and roared. Fifty yards away, Guillotine stopped rowing and stared at the dragon. Then he was busy with the net at the bottom of the skiff.

Herald Bouteille clattered to the top of the stairs and shouted at Bella:

"His Highness wishes to inform you that he does not wish his ship to be dashed to pieces on the cliffs!"

"Tell His Highness to get some guts!" Bella snapped, before she could stop herself.

The Herald looked shocked, but there was no time for apologies now. Bella turned back and tried to lasso the outcropping again. This time the hook held fast, sinking deep into the barnacles. Bella tied off the loose remaining rope and then gestured Disagree forward.

"Ah-Time!" she shouted at the helmsman, who was leaning against the aft railing, regarding everything serenely. "Get on the helm, or you will be responsible for what happens when Dis lets go!"

Startled, the helmsman ran forward just in time to take over from Disagree, who came to Bella's side and untied the rope from the cleat. He seemed to have anticipated what she was doing, and Bella was grateful. Who knew what might have happened if he hadn't taken the helm.

Dis smiled. "Don't worry. I'm always here to hold your loose ends."

Bella rolled her eyes.

"Just keep it tight, all right?" she said.

Disagree grimaced. "Go. Just don't get yourself brained, that's all."

"Maybe I'm brained already," she replied, throwing him a grin.

Leviathan roared again, and Bella looked around. Guillotine was rowing backwards, trailing the net into which Leviathan had blundered as he tried to follow. The dragon rolled and twisted. His heart-tipped tail beat the water into froth as he tried to break free from the mesh, but he succeeded only in entangling himself further. Guillotine seemed to be waiting until the dragon was thoroughly incapacitated before circling back to try to cut one of his claws.

Clever boy, Bella thought. Then, out loud, "But he'd better do it quickly." Leviathan wouldn't be trapped very long before those claws went to work and he broke free, truly enraged. And once done with Guillotine as his main course, he would be looking around for some dessert. Her advantage, real as it was, would soon vanish, leaving less than even odds. Time was short.

Touching Dis's hand in farewell, Bella grabbed the rope and leapt over the railing. She pulled herself hand over hand toward the cliff, ignoring the pain of her bruised shoulder. When the rope was taut, her feet kicked the tops of the waves. Then the ship drifted in toward the cliff, immersing her to the waist. At the helm, Disagree compensated, and she rose into the air again.

Within minutes she had reached the outcropping and was scrambling along the face of the cliff, barely aware of the barnacles that cut into her flesh and the crabs that emerged from the crevices to nip at her toes. Every few seconds, a wave hit and rose over her head. As the water rushed out of the cave, she clung to avoid being sucked back. Then she went on.

At last, as her shoulder, hands, and feet started screaming too loudly to ignore, the cliff suddenly opened. The waves ran in unabated, but from somewhere inside she heard a roar, and the cave mouth exhaled a breath of spray into the air. Fear clutched at her stomach, but she knew that hesitating now would mean facing something far more terrifying when Leviathan freed himself from the net. Taking a breath, she worked her way along the rocks and into the cave mouth.

***

On the deck of *La Justice*, Jack Hodoul had emerged from below decks with his entourage. The king now stood at the rail and regarded the mouth of the cave with an impassive calm that belied his excitement. *Bold*, he thought. *Bolder than I could have hoped, my dear.*

"He's on him!" a crewman shouted from the bows. Hodoul dragged his eyes away from the cliff. He realized that he had been gripping the rail in a manner that might raise speculations. He dropped his hands to his sides and strode across the deck. The scene there was not as intriguing as Bella's escapades, but it was certainly entertaining.

Leviathan had succeeded in entangling himself in Guillotine's net, and now the pirate had steered the skiff to within a few feet of where the dragon tossed in the waves. He stood, balancing himself in the bucking skiff, and Hodoul saw the tip and handle of the saw he had strapped to his back. Then, judging his moment, Guillotine leapt, landed on the dragon's stomach, and grabbed a fistful of netting. Leviathan roared and bucked, emitting a cloud of steam—all that sea-going dragons could manage of their airborne ancestors' flames. Guillotine stuck like a horsefly. He maneuvered himself to where Leviathan's front legs lay bound against his chest. With one hand, he untied the saw and squatted. He grabbed one of the dragon's legs, and Hodoul drew in his breath as Guillotine began to cut.

Leviathan went mad. His claws tore through the netting and flicked Guillotine backwards through the air into the waves beyond the two-hundred-yard perimeter. The dragon tore the rest of the net into shreds and smashed the skiff into kindling with his tail. Satisfied that nothing remained of the irritating opponent, he swam circles of victory, roaring and blowing steam. However, Hodoul had anticipated what would happen next. The king was already crossing to the port rail when Leviathan stopped circling, gathered himself, and made a run toward the cave, spreading a three-foot-high wake of foam and green water behind him.

Reaching the rail with his entourage straggling in tow, Hodoul leaned forward and hurled a thought toward the cave with all his strength. *Get out, Bella! Get out now!*

***

Deep within the cave, kneeling among the fish-bones and shed scales, Bella heard Leviathan roaring and guessed that Guillotine's net had met its end. Time to leave. She grabbed the smallest of the objects for which she had been searching and tied it crosswise to her back with the loose ends of her shirt. She slipped off the ledge into the water and started back toward the cave mouth. As the waves rushed in through the tunnel, they threatened to dash her back against the walls, but she timed her movements in reverse to those of her entrance, anchoring herself to a handhold on the inflow before letting go and allowing the ebb to carry her outward.

She was almost out when she saw the head of Leviathan ploughing toward her, pushing a wave before itself. She screamed, kicking and struggling, trying to angle herself away from the dragon's path, but the tow was too strong. She was going to be swept into his jaws.

She felt herself slow. The ebb of the wave that was carrying her had met the counter-wave pushed forward by the dragon. Again, she kicked and pulled with her arms, and this time she was able to drag herself to the edge of the cave's mouth. Trembling, her stomach heaving with fear, she wedged herself into the crevice between two boulders. But she was barely able to take a breath before Leviathan roared again. He had heard her scream. Halting his forward rush to confront this new intruder, he reared up, his red eyes glittering.

Following some instinct, Bella untied her prize from behind her back. Her fingers were clumsy with fear, and she only managed to get one end loose before Leviathan darted forward. Bella jumped backwards into the crevice just as the dragon's snout struck the stone in front of her. With a loud report, the rock split. As Leviathan pulled his head back to strike again, Bella untied the other end of her prize and gripped it at the base with both hands. It was a claw, about four feet long, silver and curved like a scimitar.

Leviathan's head snaked down from a higher angle. A moment before he struck, Bella threw herself backwards. His snout hit, cracking the rock in front of her again, and she stabbed the claw into his eye, the sharp edges of the base cutting into her palms. Leviathan screamed and reared back with green blood snaking from his eye. As he rose, one of his fins grazed Bella's foot, opening it in a gush of red. Bella shrieked, but her noise was drowned in the sounds of the dragon's pain. Seized by great convulsions, his body cleared the water, twisting in midair, somersaulting. Then he hit the surface in a thunderous burst of foam and steam and, with a slap of his tail, upended and dove into the depths of the sinkhole.

Bella sat staring at the place where Leviathan had dove, shaking violently, her breath coming in short gasps. Slowly, she became aware that the gale had died, leaving the water agitated but no longer tormented. On the edge of the two-hundred-yard perimeter, men lined the ships' railings, staring toward her.

She saw *Tongue of the Devil* and wondered if Guillotine had survived. Then she turned her attention to *La Justice*, where the slight figure of the king stood amidships. *He came on deck to watch*, she thought with a flicker of pride. Behind the king was Disagree. He was shouting now, and gesturing. Then he and several other crewmen lowered a skiff over the side. Disagree leapt in as soon as the hull touched the waves and drove toward her, ignoring the possibility that Leviathan might break the surface, more enraged than ever.

Same old Dis, Bella thought. *Always worrying.*

The weight of what had happened descended on her. The edges of her vision darkened. She blinked and shook her head. The darkness spread. Dizziness overcame her, and she pitched forward.

The darkness parted in flickers... Disagree rowing above her, glancing down with dark eyes... the masts of *La Justice* framing a sky torn with red clouds... Disagree again, carrying her down steps... the king's voice ordering, "You will treat her in the stateroom, doctor, in my bed"...

Disagree smiling as he laid her on something soft... a bitter, fragrant taste in her mouth...

Then darkness crashed over her. She let go and sank away into unconsciousness.

Chapter Five

Bella opened her eyes. She was lying in a bed, the white eye of the moon staring down at her, framed by the open porthole. From the way the cabin around her creaked, the regularity of the ship's movements, and the gentle *slap* of waves against the hull, she could tell they were no longer in the grip of the North Point current. They swung like a gentle pendulum, back and forth around a fixed point. She thought, *We must be anchoredin harbor. We've been back for a while.*

She sat up, examining the bandages on her hands and feet. The pain, faded now, throbbed with her heartbeat.

A voice rasped, "The salve contains a few special ingredients. Your wounds will heal in a matter of hours."

Bella peered into the far corner of the cabin from which the voice had come. A match flared, and Hodoul's tousled head appeared. He touched the unlit cigarette dangling from his lips with the match. When the tip glowed, he whipped the match out, and his face sank into an obscure dusk.

"You slept a while," he said. "Making up for a few lost years?"

For once, she found herself unable to come back with anything. A nest of snakes had come to life in her stomach. Here was the moment, and suddenly, all her planned-for sophistication vanished.

"You had a right to your sleep," the king continued. "It was a bold thing you did, Bella Couteau." He glided across the cabin to the porthole. In the moonlight, his face beneath the pile of curling silver hair was impossibly cracked and wrinkled, like a riverbed in a drought. His deadened eyes stared forward.

"Very bold," he said. "Perhaps too bold." He glanced at Bella, and she felt a film of ice creep over her skin.

"You had a plan today," Hodoul continued. "Didn't you?"

Bella said nothing. The cabin's walls seemed to be closing in on her.

"You didn't even approach the dragon. You went straight for the cave. You knew exactly where to look."

Bella's heartbeat was almost painful to endure, but she folded her arms and lifted her chin, staring at him.

"Tell me, girl!" Hodoul snapped. "How did you know?"

Bella took a deep breath. "I knew that he sheds his claws."

"And how did you know that?"

"I watched him..." She paused. "From the top of the cliffs above his run."

The king gazed at her, his eyes stony.

"Good," he said finally. "I was right about you. You are not tentative, and that is always encouraging."

As Bella struggled with his sudden change of mood, he turned from the window and sat down at the edge of the bed.

"So now you know the answer," he said.

"The answer..." Isabella said.

"To the question that everyone asks. *Where do the claws come from?*" He smiled. "Now you know the answer."

Isabella considered this. "But how does Granbousse get into the cave?"

Hodoul raised his eyebrows. "Don't the old-timers talk about how I caught the dragon in the first place?"

Isabella shook her head, and Hodoul chuckled. "Well, I put him to sleep."

Isabella gaped. "To sleep... How?"

"Ah." Hodoul touched his nose. "That's my secret. Let's just say the old Claw-man Zarastra taught me how. So, when we got Leviathan—I chose that name, by the way—when we got him back and chained him up, Granbousse and I thought we'd have to trim his claws ourselves.

And for the first few months, that's what we did. Then we discovered what you learned, and since then, it's been easy. Once he is asleep, we just go in and get what we need for the month."

"But why do you allow it?" Isabella said, with sudden boldness. "It makes people sick when they don't get enough…"

Hodoul stared at her, and she thought she had gone too far. Then he said, "Because I am a realist. Fine words and pieces of paper are all necessary, but one also needs a little incentive to keep things calm, or to help things along, or to prevent people from making decisions they might later regret…

"But," he continued, waving the previous thought aside, "those are just practical issues, the unfortunate compromises one makes to govern imperfect people. There is in fact a bigger principle here… Tell me, Bella." He leaned forward. "Do you know why I really keep Leviathan alive?"

"Because you need Claw…"

"Yes, yes. But *why*? Think bigger!"

Isabella was silent. "Perhaps you wanted to remind us…" She paused. "That *you* were the one who caught him."

The king leaned back and took a satisfied pull on his cigarette before pinching it out and flicking it out the porthole.

"Yes, I was right about you," he repeated, nodding. "You are quite right. A little inexact perhaps, but quite right. You see, Bella—may I call you that?" Bella nodded and the king continued. "Power is not the ability to destroy your enemies. What good is that, after all? Once the opponent is gone, so too is one's power over him. Real enduring power lies not in destruction but in *restraint*. A dead Leviathan is just another rotting dragon's corpse, white bones turning to dust, claws burned to smoke and inhaled and consumed and forgotten. But Leviathan bound—now that is a legacy of power that will always be remembered!" He paused, and added with a smile, "Not to mention a useful supply of claws to keep everything running smoothly…"

"Yes," Bella said, with a little more conviction than she intended.

Listening to the king, she had felt the mist inside her parting, revealing something bright and sharp, the thing she had been seeking...

"So, you understand me, then," the king said, with a trace of amusement in his voice. Bella realized she had exposed her feelings, and her cheeks burned. She glanced away and shrugged.

"I think you do. You understand, otherwise you would not have done what you did today. Most of that bunch out there—" he gestured at the door "—would kill anyone or anything in their way to get what they needed. But you understand the distinctions, the finer points. There is something—*considered* about your actions. That's why..."

He paused and fumbled in his pockets, finally pulling out a tobacco pouch. He began to roll another cigarette.

"That's why," he continued, "I chose that challenge for you."

Bella stared at him, her thoughts losing all coherence.

"I have been watching you for some time now, Bella Couteau," the pirate king said. "Ever since I... ever since you came to my island, in fact. I watched your little trips to the North Point cliffs, and I suspected that you had discovered Leviathan's secret." He laughed. "Did you think it was just some beautiful coincidence that Herald Bouteille offered the very challenge you alone were prepared to meet successfully? Please tell me you're not one of those romantic types!"

A thought flashed into Bella's mind and she spoke before she could stop herself. "So that's why the Herald looked at me like that," she said. "Because you knew I would accept the challenge!"

Hodoul inclined his head. "Very good. Yes, I told him you might well raise your hand. And you did."

"And what business is my life to you?" she asked. Bella felt deceived, caught in a plan she had known nothing about. She became aware that her medallion had slipped behind her neck, and she slipped it around again. At the same time, she felt around for the switchblade. There it was, still in the pocket of her pantaloons, beside the pouch of Claw. *It's probably all soaked and useless now*, she thought.

The king watched her with faint amusement.

"Let's just say," he said, "that I have a vested interest. All right?"

"Whatever you say," Bella said.

The king cocked his head at her. "Or perhaps I should divest myself of my interest. Should I do that, Miss Bella? If so, you could fall a long way. Or—" He paused. "I could help you rise to the heights."

There it was again—the thing she wanted glinting like a diamond unearthed in her heart, just within her grasp. With an effort, she pushed aside her anger and hurt pride and met his eyes.

"All right." She shrugged. "Tell me."

"Good," the king smiled. "Now, you have heard the name Jonah."

Bella nodded. "The tyrant of the East."

"And you remember the story of how he destroyed one of the Overlords' Trees."

Bella nodded. The story was a legend among the Brethren, retold every time they wanted to stoke their hatred of the people who lived somewhere beyond the Watchmen's line of defense.

"What you probably don't know," the king continued, "is that Jonah was no great warrior with some unknown magic at his command. He was just a boy, and he came empty-handed." Hodoul shook his head, as if unable to believe it. "More than that, Jonah came looking for his father, who was imprisoned in the Tree. And do you know what he did? He offered to take his father's place *for free!*" The king nodded at Bella's shocked expression. "And that's what did it."

"Just that?" Bella said, incredulous.

"Yes. Because he did not sell himself to the Djinn, he was free, and the Tree could not contain him."

Bella was silent, trying to catch a thought in the storm of speculations that whirled around in her head. The king sucked on his cigarette and exhaled, all the time watching her through the billows of moonlit smoke. The cracks and wrinkles in his face seemed deeper in the shadows.

Bella returned his gaze, thinking hard. *What does he want?*

"The simple fact is, I can't continue allowing this boy to rule the

People of the Wind," the king said. "They say he is even more of a child than his age. A fool, slightly." He tapped his head with one finger. "And yet they maintain some sort of absurd loyalty to him, more even perhaps than the previous old fool commanded." His voice now took on a derisive edge that Bella had never heard before. "He has inculcated with them with the insane belief that the more hopeless, hapless, and pathetic a person, the more worthy of reverence he is!"

Suddenly restless, Hodoul stood. He struck a match and lit a lamp on the bedside table. When the flame was burning evenly and an olive light touched the corners of the room, he met her eyes again.

"You would think, would you not, that such folly would pose no problem for those of us who live under the assurance of law and order, but it is not so. In the past year, I have intercepted no fewer than five defectors who had somehow allowed themselves to imagine that the tyrant's *slavery*—" his voice rose "—was somehow preferable over freedom and power. Can you imagine?"

Bella shook her head, remembering how even that morning she had speculated about life with the People of the Wind. It was a shameful memory, and she pushed it away, focusing on the king again.

"Exactly," he declared. "I had to subject those traitors to some unpleasant forms of persuasion, just so that their treachery might be concealed, at least until I have solved the Jonah problem."

Bella thought, *Here it comes.*

"Then one day, the solution came at last to me," the king said. "And you were the first person I thought about."

"What was it?" Bella asked. It felt as if her heart had come loose in her chest.

The king smiled. "I thought, *she would make the perfect deserter.*"

Bella's eyes widened. "You want me to pretend that I deserted the Brethren?"

"Yes," the king nodded. "And then?"

"And when I am there..." Bella's voice failed on her. She made an effort and managed, "You want me to—"

Hodoul smiled. "Yes."

"But how?" she said. "They won't believe me."

Hodoul's eyes crinkled, but he did not smile. "I leave that to your expertise."

"I'm not good at pretending."

"Oh, I think you are," the king replied. "More than you imagine. Besides," he said, glancing away at the door again, "you may find a motive yet. Sometimes help comes from unexpected places."

"I don't know," Bella said, a faint panic taking hold of her.

Hodoul sighed. "Well, I am afraid your uncertainty is a luxury you can no longer afford. Bouteille!" he called.

The door opened. Orange lamplight spilled in from the passageway, outlining the shape of Herald Bouteille.

"Tell Monsieur Granbousse to calm down at last," Hodoul said. "I will hear his complaint in a few minutes."

"Very well, Majesty," Bouteille said, and closed the door.

A coldness flooded Bella's stomach. *He knew... Dis was right...*

Hodoul turned back to her. "He has been pestering me ever since this morning. Perhaps you can tell me why?"

Bella clenched her jaw and said nothing.

Hodoul reached out his hand. "Give it to me."

"Give what?" Isabella said.

"You know very well!" Hodoul said. "Give me whatever is left of the package. We have to make the best of it now!"

Isabella reached into her pocket and pulled out the package of Claw. Hodoul took it. He paused in the doorway and looked back at her one more time. She couldn't see his expression—his face was hidden in the shadows—but the lamplight ignited the pile of curls around his head. Then he closed the door without a word. For some reason, that hurt her more than anything he might have said.

Bella slipped out of bed, her thoughts fluttering around in her mind like trapped birds. She considered trying to escape. There was no way through the door—too many guards stood between her and the deck.

The cabin porthole was too small, even for her skinny frame... She had no choice but to face Granbousse. And who knew how Hodoul would "make the best" of that?

In the stifling heat, she was shivering.

Chapter Six

Bella stood alone in a space on the main deck, surrounded by the crew of *La Justice*. The other ships, lit with lanterns and torches, floated as close as they dared, their railings lined with men who strained to catch a word or a glimpse. Clouds had drifted over the moon, and now the full weight of midnight pressed down on them, held at bay only by the torches set up around the deck. The wind whistled and moaned in the loose rigging.

Before Bella sat Hodoul on a low carved stool, with Disagree planted immobile behind him. The flat canvas pouch of Claw rested in the king's hands. His face was inscrutable as he examined it. To one side stood the pear-shaped figure of Joe Granbousse, while Apoojamy's head bobbed in and out from behind his master's bulk. Joe was grinning like a furious gargoyle.

The king broke the silence. "You are certain this is your merchandise?"

"Whose else?" Joe snorted. "It be my oilskin and everything! And if His Majesty be trying to cast doubt—"

"All right," the king snapped. "We were just asking." He looked up at Bella for the first time. His eyes were stones.

"Foolish of the thief not to dispose of incriminating evidence," he murmured. "Foolish and really quite disappointing." Bella did not lower her gaze, but her insides coiled into tighter knots.

"What do you have to say for yourself, Sister Couteau?" the king asked.

Bella looked at him wordlessly. She knew what she wanted to

say—*the fat pig deserved to be robbed blind*—but she knew that it would make no difference now. She had failed her test.

She shook her head.

The king's mouth twisted. "Very well then. Let the law be read!"

Herald Bouteille elbowed his way out of the crowd behind the king, bearing a golden scroll before him like a standard. Strutting to the center of the deck, he pushed Bella aside. He unrolled the scroll with a sweeping gesture, tilted his head, cleared his throat, and began to read in a funereal voice, quite different from the chant he had used to issue the challenge that morning:

"Hear ye Hodoul's Law of the Brethren, as has been taught and handed down from the beginning in word and deed, and hereon inscribed in gold and for everlasting time by His Majesty, Hodoul, king of the Brethren. These laws were and are and shall ever be binding on all who call themselves Brethren; that is, all who have thrown off the shackles of the Wind and its minion, the so-called Elder of the East—" a cheer went up from the men at these words "—and who now live for freedom by a strong hand and a cunning mind.

"In the first, be it known that all the Brethren shall obey their own captain. Disobedience is punishable by hanging. In the second, be it known that all the Brethren shall pay tribute to the king and to their own captain. The former shall receive a quarter of each share of prizes, the latter an eighth. Withholding prizes from the authorities is punishable by hanging or marooning. In the third, be it known that deserters will be marooned or hanged. In the fourth, be it known that thieves from among the Brethren will be marooned or hanged..." Fear clutched Bella harder. Joe's grin widened.

"That's enough," the king said. Herald Bouteille looked disappointed but knew better than to object. He rolled up the scroll, bowed to the king, glanced at Bella, and retreated into the crowd. Silence fell, made heavier by the slap of waves on the hull. The torch flames rippled over the faces of the men around her, the lines of their faces traced harshly one moment, smoothed the next, eyes exposed and glittering, then hidden again in darkness.

"By the fourth, I want justice!" Joe Granbousse declared. "Let her be—"

"We will pass the sentence, thank you very much!" the king snapped.

"I be having the right—"

"No, you do not! You may have certain privileges amongst the men, but we are the king and we will dispense justice!"

Joe opened his mouth to reply, then closed it. He shifted with frustration, mopping his forehead with a filthy kerchief.

Hodoul leaned back. "Sister Couteau, stand forward."

Wishing she could curl up and disappear, Bella squared her shoulders and met the king's eyes without flinching.

"We must repeat our disappointment," the king said softly. "Your actions today were worthy of all honor. We expected to commend you, to raise you above your low estate—" he emphasized the last words "—but instead, we must punish you for breaking the law. It would seem that meritorious actions should cancel crimes, but it is not so. The law is the law and must be upheld, for without this is darkness and anarchy." He paused. "Therefore, for thieving Monsieur Granbousse's merchandise, you will be marooned in the realm of the Blind Watchmen."

Joe chortled, and a murmur broke out among the men. Bella could hear voices calling the verdict from ship to ship.

"Your Majesty." Disagree spoke for the first time, leaning forward. He had turned grey. "A word with you." The king raised his hand without turning and raised his voice to continue. "However."

Joe's grin faltered and silence fell.

"We believe that some recognition must be offered for this girl's bravery today. We have decreed marooning in accordance with the law. This is *not* a death sentence." He paused. "And if our Sister should survive the depredations of the monster and somehow return to us, her debt shall be nullified." He raised his voice over the murmuring that had broken out. "She shall return to her former condition, blameless, holding all of the rights she has lost today, including—" he looked at Bella directly now, pinning her "—the honor she has rightly earned."

It's a reprieve, Bella thought wildly. *And if I can get through... !* Her mind spun. The fear that had paralyzed her now began thrashing around in her stomach, as if searching for a way out. Hearing the conversation rippling through the crowd around her and on the other ships, she knew that the king had scored a coup. The men were going for it. After all, the decision made sense—it was just. Only Joe stared at the king with bewilderment spread across his face. He could not turn the tide of approval, but she knew he could be a real obstruction.

She waited. The king seemed to be waiting too. He was leaning back, watching Joe through lowered lids.

The merchant roused himself and looked around. He seemed to realize the mood of the crowd, and swung his head from side to side. Then he took a step forward and the noise faded away.

"It is not lawful for her to have any help," he declared.

"Ah, give over, Granbousse!" someone shouted.

"Yeah, Joe, leave it alone!"

The king regarded Joe. "We know the law," he said. "We wrote it."

Joe's eyes narrowed. "So, she will be alone?"

"Of course."

"Your word before witnesses?"

"Our word."

"Pah!" Joe Granbousse spat in disgust. "Then your so-called generosity be meaningless! If she survives, I'll be kissing her hand myself and giving her a lifetime of my best Claw. Guaranteed!"

The king shrugged. "If you say so, Joe."

Joe spat again and pushed away through the crowd, shouting, "Lower a boat. I be having real work to do!" Apoojamy threw Bella a glance of prim triumph and scurried off in his master's wake.

"Clear the ships!" the king shouted. "Monsieur Disagree, you will stay at our side. Herald Bouteille!"

"Yes, Majesty?"

"Two rounds of rum from our personal stores for every man tonight."

A cheer went up. The Herald looked surprised. "You are staying, Majesty?"

"Yes. At daybreak, send a crew to sail east for the marooning."

Half an hour later, the last skiff pulled away toward the shore. *La Justice* was deserted, except for Bella and Disagree, who had not moved from their positions. King Hodoul, who now stood at the starboard rail with his hands behind his back, watched the departing boats.

"Monsieur Disagree," the king said. "Please take the condemned below and lock her in my cabin."

"Your Majesty," Disagree said. "I beg you."

"I need to speak with you alone, Dis. Please do as I say."

Bella glanced at her friend's face as they went below, but he looked straight ahead as they wove their way aft through the dim passage until they reached the master's cabin door. As Disagree pushed it open, he spoke. "Next time you listen to me. All right?"

"Dis, it's fine, really," Bella said. "I can do this—"

"You think you can survive the Blind Watchmen?" Disagree shouted. "No one done it before, in the whole history of the Brethren. From the beginning! And you think you, fifteen years old, you can do it?"

"Why not?" Bella lifted her chin. "I got Leviathan, didn't I?"

Disagree shook his head. "What kind of head do you have on you? Do you see this monster?"

"Yes, I've seen him. So?"

"Fine," Disagree said. "If you don't live with your head straight, then you be someone else's food!"

"Fine!" Bella stormed into the cabin and slammed the door behind her. "Nothing like the confidence of a friend!" she screamed from inside.

Disagree sighed and pressed his fingers into his eyes before going back up on deck.

Hodoul was leaning against the railing with a cigarette lit. He flicked the cigarette into the dark water. "Hello, my friend."

Disagree inclined his head. "Majesty," he said. "I cannot allow this."

The king nodded. "I know. Nor can I. You know that."

"Then—why do you—"

"Because she left the compound without permission," the king snapped, "and she foolishly stole Granbousse's product without doing what any sensible pirate would do—bury it somewhere until things cooled down!"

"She's young," Disagree said, after a moment of silence.

"I know," Hodoul sighed. "But I have to abide by my own law, Dis. I may be a king, but even I have no choice in that."

"Then what to do?"

"Nothing. *I* can do nothing."

"Then I desert," Disagree declared. "I do not let her die alone."

The king nodded. "Yes," he said slowly. "You must do as you see fit. For my part, of course, I will utterly deny having heard what you just said, which will be easy, since we have no witnesses."

Disagree stared at him.

"Is that why you do not let me speak back then?" he asked.

The king inclined his head.

"But if I come back with her, I am a traitor—"

The king smiled. "It will be one of my few acts of mercy. One, I think, that few would contest."

Disagree looked doubtful. "Granbousse maybe."

The king made a dismissive gesture. "Be discreet, that's all. Joe is far stupider than we can imagine."

Disagree was silent.

"Suppose the monster get the better of us?" he asked.

The king laughed and clapped his shoulder. "Go ashore, Dis. Make sure that we have a few sober men for tomorrow. I don't trust that Herald. I sometimes wonder if he's missing a few essentials."

As Disagree pulled away in a skiff, he looked up to where Hodoul leaned against the aft railing. A lamp hung from the yardarm transformed the king's hair into silver flames. His face lay in pitch darkness.

"One way or another, you must take care of her, Dis," the king said softly. "With your life, if necessary."

"Always, Your Majesty," Dis replied. "Always I die a thousand times a day inside for that little one."

Chapter Seven

Waves unrolled before the bow like ruffles on a blue silk sheet. Neither the trails of cloud streaming overhead nor the single foresail to maintain the ship's momentum succeeded in sheltering the main deck from the molten heat. Against the railing a few idle deckhands wilted, with dark sweat patches blooming on their filthy shifts and stained pantaloons. Despite their languor, however, their bodies held a listening stillness as they peered ahead—watching for something.

Bella, Disagree, and Hodoul waited at the bow. The king sat on his low stool, sheltered by the only available shade—a canvas umbrella propped behind him. Bella stood with the straightness of someone trying to fight back the weight of the sun with her body, clenching the rail with both hands and looking as if something inside her were freezing over. To her left, Disagree was a sweating mountain. Occasionally, he moved his eyes over her face, and when she did not acknowledge him, he glanced toward the king, who smiled but said nothing.

"Sandbar!" The lookout's voice, thin and ragged, floated down from the mast.

Hodoul stood. "Where away?" he shouted.

"Three points off the port bow!"

The king squinted at the horizon, then looked at Disagree. Disagree nodded marginally. His face was granite.

"Make for the sandbar!" The king called back at the helm. "And throw up a topsail," he added to one of the hands. The man immediately scrambled up the mast. As a bright triangle bloomed above them, Hodoul strolled to where Bella stood. "It's time, my dear," he murmured.

Bella clenched her jaw and her hands, staring ahead.

"Don't make this unseemly," the king said. "It would not be worthy of you."

Bella turned to face him. "That bastard deserved to lose everything he had."

Hodoul's lips twisted. "Well, that's the beauty of the law. It is ignorant of human feelings."

"What about everything else you said?" Bella demanded. "Meaningless?"

The king shrugged. "Perhaps I misjudged."

"You didn't!"

"Then prove it."

Bella broke his gaze at last and cast her eyes to the main deck. The crew's eyes were fixed on her.

"I will," she said. She strode amidships. The king threw a half-smile at Disagree as they followed her back.

"Launch the skiff!" Hodoul shouted. "Move, you dogs!"

Several hands scurried to man the ropes, hoisting the skiff into the air, swinging it over and down to the water. Bella leapt in, and the king tossed a gunny sack down to her. It contained a loaf of bread, a full skin bottle, and a pistol loaded with a single shot—the traditional supplies for one of the Brethren who was to be marooned. In addition, the sack held a roll of coarse twine.

Hodoul now trained a pistol on her.

"If you would not mind..." he said.

"I've got it!" Bella snapped. She was already in the bottom of the boat, trying to tie the loose end of the twine to the drain plug ring. When the bandages on her hands came loose and entangled the knot, she swore and ripped them off. Seeing that the dragon claw wounds had healed as the king had promised, Bella unwrapped her feet, then finished tying the knot. She hurled the rest of the twine at Disagree's face. He dodged it, the hurt almost hidden in the depths of his eyes.

"Monsieur Disagree," the king said. "If you would do the honors."

Disagree's eyes flared, and he opened his mouth to protest. The king looked at him, and the flame in Disagree's eyes went out. He bent and picked up the twine, enclosing it in one immense fist.

The king turned back to Bella. She had settled herself at the oars, looking up at them, pale and defiant.

The king raised his hand in a gentle salute. "Farewell, my dear," he said softly.

"I'll be back," she retorted.

"That remains to be seen," he replied.

Bella looked at Disagree, but he seemed to have shrunk into himself, leaving a mountainous husk behind. Her voice struggled, trying to get past her lips and reach him, but she forced herself to hold it.

"It is time to go, Bella," the king said. "And don't try to untie the rope, or I will have to shoot you."

Bella kept her eyes fixed on Disagree, but he was far away from her now, and tears filled her eyes. *Damn you, Couteau!* she screamed at herself, blinked hard, and pulled away from *La Justice*. As she rowed, the frail umbilical cord of the twine unrolled slowly from Disagree's fist, while he, the king, and the crew watched her, observing the silence due the condemned.

Any moment now, Bella thought. Looking over her shoulder, she could make out waves breaking on the sandbar.

The king nodded at Disagree, then turned away. Disagree, his face almost grey, crushed the ball in his fist. In the skiff, the twine came taut, jerking the drain plug from the hull with a loud *pop*. The plug and twine dropped over the side into the ocean. Warm water flooded in, and Bella strained hard at the oars.

The sea turned from blue to transparent. She could see the white sand bottom with strands of seaweed waving in the current. A hermit crab in a conch scurried for cover from a shoal of angelfish.

The water in the skiff now swirled around her calves. The hull grew heavy and sluggish in her hands. Above, the weight of the sun and the washed-out blue sky pressed down on her shoulders. Sweat poured in rivulets down her face and into her eyes as she dragged the craft forward.

The hull touched the bottom, then slid on, slowing rapidly. Bella rowed on, sitting in a pond of warm seawater with the gunny sack perched on her knees. A moment later, a crunching sound—the skiff had come aground. Clutching the sack, Bella waded to the bow and, balancing on the gunwale, leapt the last two yards onto a sandbar no larger than a standard doorway.

The sandbar would be her home until the currents washed it away. *Or until the Blind Watchman comes...* She pushed the thought out of her mind. Out in the deep water, *La Justice* was already rounding for home. They could not risk waiting this close to the Blind Watchman's realm. The mainsail was set, and fore and topsails bloomed with every second until she was heeling under the breeze, spreading a wake through the clear water.

At the aft railing, the great black figure of Disagree stood looking back at Bella. She could still feel his eyes from this distance and fought to keep from raising her hand. Then he shrank as the schooner carried him away. The hull dropped out of sight. The white triangles of the sails rested on the horizon, then sank away.

Bella stared at the place where *La Justice* had been. She reached into the gunny sack for the pistol. She examined it, ornate and glinting in the sunlight. She knew it held a single discharge for the moment when she wanted to be free from suffering. Or else, she thought, a single shot to kill the Blind Watchman. She grimaced and shivered at the same time. One way or another, she would need that discharge.

She wrapped the pistol in the loose hem of her shirt, knotting the ends to secure it. Setting her face against the emptiness of ocean and sky, feeling lost inside herself, Bella sat down to wait for death.

Chapter Eight

Bella scraped the mold off the end of the loaf and took a measured bite. She resisted the urge to stuff in the last mouthful. Chewing the bread more than she needed to, she held up the wineskin, now shrunken, and shook it. She could no longer hear the contents. Probably two or three mouthfuls left, she estimated. No more than two days. It was almost over, either way.

"Good," she muttered. "This place is getting really boring."

***

The fire of thirst woke her. As she forced her swollen tongue across her mouth, her lips cracked—salty blood on her tongue. She sat up, squinting against the light that seemed brighter today. A few feet away, a hermit crab scurried across the sand, naked without its shell. Bella untied her shirt and freed the pistol. With the butt reversed, she snapped her arm forward, and the hermit lay crushed on the sand, its legs kicking toward the sky. Bella ate the crab on her hands and knees, feeding on the raw morsels of its flesh and sucking every drop of its fluids.

"I am sorry, my friend," she whispered. "It was you or me."

Later that day, she saw something bobbing near the edge of the shallows. She waded out into the warm turquoise water and almost wept to find a coconut. Using the skiff's prow, she succeeded in husking and breaking it open, salvaging a couple of mouthfuls of milk from the cracks before it drained onto the sand. The meat, scraped off with a shell, was achingly sweet and cool on her tongue. She took her time to eat, but still it was gone too soon.

"One more day," she whispered. In response, the sea glittered and exhaled on her a gust of damp salt.

***

Wind roared overhead during the night. Bella opened her eyes, and darkness pressed into her. The images of half-sleep—Disagree smiling, Leviathan snaking down toward her—receded.

Perhaps it will rain, she thought. *Just in time.*

Something slammed down, as if a door had fallen on her, driving the breath from her lungs. As she struggled to turn over, suffocating in the stench of goat and decaying bodies, a hand, hard as petrified wood, closed around her and jerked her into the air.

Bella struggled with the last of her strength. The monster's grip tightened. A rumbling came over the wind. "Don't bother, Pretty." The blood throbbed in Bella's forehead. Consciousness faded.

Chapter Nine

Water rushed down over her head, cool and sweet. Bella struggled out of the hole in her mind, aware of a smooth rock beneath her and wind streaming over her skin. Somewhere nearby, coconut fronds rattled.

The Blind Watchman's voice came again, like the sound of a collapsing cliff. "Wake up, Pretty." And again, the water poured down. This time she turned and lifted her mouth to the solid stream, coughing and spluttering with each swallow until her stomach was tight and painfully full.

She opened her eyes and pushed herself upright. The eyeless face of the Blind Watchman stared at her through a row of solid wooden bars. Perched on a ledge, her cage was a cube of takamaka poles lashed with thick ropes. A giant coconut tree threw patterns of noon sunlight over the ledge. Below and surrounding her on all sides, the ocean spread and receded to blue infinity.

"Nowhere to go, Pretty," the Blind Watchman said, with a breath of abscessed teeth that smelled like a dead body. "Those ropes are stronger than me."

A panic seized Bella. She felt around for her possessions. They were all gone—the pistol, the switchblade, even her medallion. Bella scrambled forward and slammed the bars with her fists.

"Where are my things?" she shouted.

The Blind Watchman chuckled. "After I am done, Pretty won't need them anymore. I will keep them safe for the little pirate!"

"But I'm not a pirate!" Bella said desperately. "Not anymore."

"They marooned her, eh?" The Blind Watchman grinned. "Poor Pretty!"

"Stop calling me Pretty!" Bella snapped, touching the blond tangle of her hair. "You're blind anyway!"

"I felt that she's a girl and I hope she's pretty," the Blind Watchman replied. "Either way, she needs a bath!"

"You can talk," Bella retorted.

The Blind Watchman chortled. "It's my memories, Pretty. Memories of meals gone by!" There was a loud *snap*. A coconut dropped from the tree and bounced off the top of the cage. The Blind Watchman caught the nut in midair, cracked it like an egg against the ledge, and handed it through.

"A snack to fatten her up," he grinned.

Bella scooped the meat out, filling her mouth. She could already feel new strength seeping through her.

"Eating people is disgusting," she declared, when she had finished.

"So *she* says," the Blind Watchman replied. "I call it service to the Wind. Ridding the world of dirty things!"

A squawk cut in. "Sophistry!"

Bella looked up. A giant parrot sat at the peak of the cage, its charcoal feathers glinting in the sunlight. The bird's head was tilted to one side, regarding the Blind Watchman with a bright eye.

The Blind Watchman did not bother to raise his head. "Crato and his big words again," he said to Bella. "Always trying to make up for his size by using words longer than he is. Poor little Polly!"

"Oh yes, three syllables," the parrot exclaimed. "So big! Well, since it seems to challenge your intellect, let me offer you a little definition. Sophistry is the habit of using elegant words and phrases to conceal immoral behavior—such as the habit of eating human flesh. And as for being *poor*," it continued, "I must be poor indeed to be friends with a thing like you!"

The Blind Watchman waved. "Ah! Admit it—what would you rather be doing than scolding me?"

"Probably enjoying a nice overripe mango on The Elder's Island."

"Now who's lying?" the Blind Watchman chortled. "Nothing's sweeter for a little bird than to feel bigger than a Blind Watchman!"

Bella interrupted, "Perhaps you two should go and argue somewhere else."

The Blind Watchman faced her. "Now look what you've done, Crato! You've made Pretty want to get eaten sooner."

Bella made her voice as calm as she could. "If you're going to eat me, then do it and stop playing games."

"Well said, well said!" Crato squawked.

"Not yet, Pretty." The Blind Watchman shook his tangled curls. "Too scrawny yet for a good meal. A few more days of coconuts and roasted fish, and I can enjoy her best. Until then, she must be patient. Now," he said, "what does she say to a nice red snapper sprinkled with sea salt, hmm?"

"You can shove your red snapper," Bella replied.

The parrot clicked its beak in disapproval, and the Blind Watchman wagged his finger. "Tsk, tsk. Pretty needs a bath on the inside too, I think. Too bad. Well, we'll see if she changes her mind when she gets a whiff of roasting fish in her nostrils! I'll be back," he said to Crato. "You keep a watch on her, old friend. Not to show pity, now!" His head disappeared below the ledge. A few minutes later, Bella saw him wading waist deep in the blue ocean. He stopped, his head swinging, listening. Then he moved on to the left, stopped, listened some more. Then he waded out, further and further, until he was a mere speck on the glittering expanse.

Bella looked up at Crato. The parrot watched her with his head cocked to one side.

"Can you help me?" she said.

The parrot cracked its beak and ruffled its feathers. "I wish I could, my dear. I really wish I could. But there are moral considerations. On the one hand, my friend's behavior, indefensible indeed; on the other hand, the greater evil of releasing you. Who knows what havoc you might wreak, what seeds of confusion you might sow, and the People are weak enough as it is."

"But I'm escaping," Bella interrupted. "I can't be all bad."

Crato cocked his head to the other side.

"They marooned me because I wouldn't follow their stupid Code," Bella continued, gratified to hear the real bitterness in her tone. "I'm sick of that life. Nothing but fighting and drinking and getting drugged all the time." *I'm good,* she thought. *I'm almost believing it myself.*

"Disgruntled pirate, eh?" Crato whistled. "I saw it once before. *Once.* And he turned out, though not without his own struggles, all of which seem to prove the rule that you can rarely trust a pirate. And even if you are sincere, experience has taught me that disgruntled persons are always so, no matter in what company they may find themselves. After all, my dear, do you imagine there are no rules among the People? If you think so, you will be sorely disillusioned. There are rules, some of them more difficult than those you are accustomed to."

"I don't care," Bella said. "I just want a new life." *Was that too much?*

Crato shifted from one foot to the other and craned his head out to sea. The Blind Watchman had moved in closer to shore. He spread his arms, and a net sailed into the air, breaking the water as it hit.

Sensing the parrot wavering and realizing she did not have much time, Bella filled her voice with as much pleading as she could. "Please, sir. Don't let me die before I can change my life."

"I don't know..." Crato's head turned left and right, as if seeking a way out. "I would need a guarantee."

"I swear—"

"Not enough!" the parrot snapped. "I would absolutely require a third party—"

A familiar voice interrupted. "I guarantee her."

"Dis!" Bella spun around and dove against the bars. He was squatting beside the coconut tree, his black face impassive as always. As he reached out his hands to grip hers, she wrinkled her nose.

"You smell like a toilet. Worse!"

Dis grinned. "I swim here so he can't smell me come. Then I wait and watch. I see where he goes to the head, you know, near his cave. It's the only way I can get in here without him knowing."

Bella looked aghast. "You mean that you put his... on your skin?!"

"Who are you, sir?" Crato demanded, his feathers ruffling to double his size. "Declare yourself immediately!"

"Calm down. He's my friend," Bella said.

"Calm down!" screeched the parrot. "Another pirate intrudes and you ask me to calm down. And he's the one you would offer as a guarantee? Laughable! One liar offering his word for another."

"Don't you dare call my friend a liar!" Bella shouted.

"Hah!" the parrot scoffed. "And why not? Did you ever hear of an honest pirate?"

"Bella!" Disagree hissed. "The Blind Watchman!"

Below, Bella saw the Blind Watchman, now standing motionless in the water, his head turned to face them.

"Damn," Bella whispered. She turned to Disagree. "Do something."

Disagree raised one hand to the parrot. "Now listen, my friend. Just listen."

"Listen?" Crato hopped from one foot to the other. "Listen to what? And don't call me your friend!"

Below, the Blind Watchman had begun wading back toward the island, kicking up waves with every stride.

"A trade," Disagree said. "I want a trade. Me for her."

"What?" Bella cried.

Crato stared down with his beak half-open. He looked as if he had been killed and stuffed on the spot.

"You want to take her place?" The parrot's words emerged as a whistle.

Disagree nodded. "I stay. She go home. My word on that."

"Dis, no!" Bella said. "I won't do it!"

"You go back," Disagree said. "The king forgive you."

"But I have things to do first!"

"What things?" Crato interrupted. "Mischief? Is that it?"

Bella glanced up at the parrot and then back at Disagree.

"I just don't want to go back," she said.

"Your choice," Dis replied. "You stay here, if you want."

Bella gaped at him. "You'd rather see me *eaten* than go on?"

Disagree shrugged. "As I say—your choice."

"Crato!" the Blind Watchman bellowed from below. "What's up there?"

"Decide now," Disagree said to Bella.

Bella glared at him and gritted her teeth.

"Fine," she said.

"Okay?" Disagree looked up at Crato.

The parrot hesitated, then twitched and stretched his head over the ledge.

"Nothing!" he squawked. "Nothing's up here!"

"Something wrong," the Blind Watchman said. "Something wrong in your voice!"

The sound of rocks tumbling against each other rose up at them.

"He's coming, by the Wind!" Crato moaned. "Oh, I knew this was unsound. I knew it from the beginning!"

Disagree was already squatting, getting his weight under the wooden bars. As he took up the strain, his face grew blacker and sinews stood out on his neck. The bottomless cage rose a few inches off the ledge. Crato squawked and flapped into the air, rising to perch at the top of the coconut tree.

"Now," he grunted. "Slide out."

Bella found herself shaking. "I can't," she said. "I can't let you do this."

Disagree swore and pushed the cage up several more inches, then slipped under before releasing his hold. As the cage crashed down, Disagree immediately enfolded Bella in his arms. Overwhelmed by the stench that covered his body, Bella held her breath, trying to control her gag reflex. Then the Blind Watchman's head rose above the ledge, his eyebrows condensed.

He sniffed and recoiled. "Crato!"

"Yes?" Crato's voice, sounding timid, floated down from the top of the tree.

"Get your tail down here!"

The parrot, looking distinctly ruffled and nervous, perched at the peak of the cage.

"Where's Pretty?" the Blind Watchman demanded.

Crato looked down to where Disagree crouched over Bella, shielding her from the Blind Watchman's nose at the back of the cage.

"What do you mean?" the parrot sounded confused. "She is still there. And—"

"And what?"

"Her... friend," stuttered the parrot. "He came to rescue her, but then he went in with her instead and..."

The Blind Watchman leaned forward and sniffed, then tilted his face up at Crato. "Are you playing games with me, Crato?"

"No, they're in there. Both of them! Say something!" Crato shouted down at Bella and Disagree.

Disagree smiled at Bella and touched his finger to his lips. Bella nodded and stuck her tongue out at Crato.

"You let them out," the Blind Watchman said. "Didn't you?"

"No!" the parrot shrieked.

"Tell me the truth!"

"I swear they're in there! Say something, you degenerates!"

"Then why can't I smell her?"

"Because her friend rolled in your filth, and you can't smell either of them under your own disgusting stink!"

The Blind Watchman considered this for a moment. Disagree gave Bella a look that said, *Get ready, any moment now.*

"There's only one way to find out," the Blind Watchman declared, and lifted the cage aside, Crato fluttering upward.

"Now," Disagree muttered, and they both scrambled backwards as the Blind Watchman' free hand swept over the ledge.

"So then, where is she?" the Blind Watchman roared.

"They're out! They're out!" Crato shrieked. "Oh, you idiot!"

Bella and Disagree slipped round the back of the tree, where fallen coconuts lay scattered at the base of the trunk. Disagree handed her a smaller-sized nut, just big enough to get her fingers around.

"Go for the middle of his face," he murmured. "It's soft."

The Blind Watchman, still feeling around on the ledge for Bella, lifted his head sharply.

"Who's that?" he shouted.

"I told you, you fool," shrieked Crato, darting in crazy circles. "It's her friend, it's her treacherous friend!"

The Blind Watchman tossed the cage away down the slope and groped around the tree, trying to get at Bella and Disagree. But his body was positioned awkwardly, and they easily dodged his clutches. He roared in frustration, grabbing the tree to pull himself closer. As he did so, Disagree drew a tiny dagger from his pantaloons and buried it in the monster's finger. The Blind Watchman screamed and slid back down the slope, losing the ground he had gained. He ripped the dagger out, sucked his finger, and pinched off the blood before scrambling upwards again.

"Hit him before he gets up!" Disagree shouted. With a coconut in each hand, he ran out onto the ledge, Bella following closely behind. At that moment, Crato swooped down at them, flapping in their faces, pecking at Disagree's head while hurling abuse in words that multiplied syllables and obscured meanings by the moment. Bella darted around the parrot, her throwing arm cocked. Reaching the edge, she saw the pile of tumbled rocks that was the island below her, the waves exploding green and white, and several abandoned boats with oars or tattered sails strewn above the break line. Then the Blind Watchman's face rose into her vision.

"There you are, Pretty!" he cried. "Nice to smell you again!"

Ignoring the stench that threatened to stupefy her and dull her movements, Bella whipped the coconut into the monster's face. It struck dead center with a dull, slightly wet sound.

The Blind Watchman stopped. He reached up with both hands and caressed the indentation. He swayed on his feet, and his hands dropped to his sides. Smoothly, Bella hurled her second coconut. For a moment, the Blind Watchman had a grotesque coconut-eye. Then the nut fell away and the Blind Watchman collapsed backwards with blood streaming from his face. His legs gave way, and he tumbled at an angle down the slope, his arms splaying in all directions. Rolling through and crushing several boats at the water's edge, he came to rest with his body half in and half out of the breakers.

Behind her, Crato let up his attack on Disagree. He swooped over Bella's head and down to perch on the monster's chest, pecking at him, trying to rouse him, incoherent with grief. Disagree, dabbing at his bleeding head, came up beside Bella, and they watched the parrot mourn.

"Is he dead?" Bella asked. The rush of energy in her blood was ebbing.

Disagree nodded. The parrot's cries had faded. He now wandered in circles over the Blind Watchman, his body hunched.

"Everyone has someone who love them," Disagree said. "Even that one."

The words disturbed Bella, but she dismissed them with a shrug.

"You watch yourself again."

She could feel Disagree's eyes. "What?"

"I think you know. You watch yourself from the outside and pretend."

"I don't care what you think I am," Bella replied. "I fixed the monster, once and for all. The king will be happy. So, whatever you think I'm pretending, it's all good enough for me!"

Disagree was regarding the parrot and the Blind Watchman again.

"So, you go back then?" he asked. "To the king?"

Bella folded her arms and turned her eyes to the horizon. "I can't."

"I know you do this," Disagree declared. "I know you go back on your word."

"I didn't go back on anything!" Bella shouted. "I stayed in the cage, didn't I?"

"So, what's so important to go on?" Disagree said angrily.

She clenched her jaw and fixed her attention on the horizon. He waited.

"Just something I need to do," she muttered.

"For him?"

"Yes."

"Huh!" Disagree shook his head. "Prove yourself again. Good for you!"

"Shut up!" Bella said. "I have to do it."

"No. He say if you survive the monster, you can come back."

Bella shook her head, her eyes full of tears now. "That's not enough. He wanted more for me than that."

Disagree sighed and shook his head. "Always more, it seems. Well, I don't stop you. I do what I need to."

Bella glanced sideways. "You didn't need to come."

"Yes, I do. He *tell* me to."

"The king told you?" Bella forgot her anger at this information. *He wanted me to escape the Blind Watchman! He wants me to go on to The Elder's Island!* A flame of confidence flared to life inside her.

She wiped her eyes of the tears that had threatened to rob her of control.

"He wants you back," Disagree said. "What else do you want now?"

She regarded him calmly now. "Just this one more thing, Dis."

"And you don't tell me what is it?"

"I can't say until it's done." Bella looked at him. "Try to understand."

Disagree was silent with disapproval.

"Go, then," he said. "But I go home now. Perhaps I see you one day. On top of the earth or under the earth, who knows?"

Disagree rinsed himself off at the water's edge. They picked their way along the shore, examining the abandoned boats. Disagree chose a light skiff whose sail was almost intact, Bella a single-outrigger canoe with a ragged lateen. They loaded their respective boats with coconuts. Neither of them spoke, though Bella occasionally threw covert glances at Disagree, wondering when he was going to try for the last word. But Disagree had sunk into himself, and he maintained the silence of an extinct volcano.

When the tree was stripped of nuts and they each had a fair supply, Disagree inclined his head at her and led the way up the slope. The Blind Watchman's lair was a long, low hollow among the rocks. From the ceiling hung coir ropes of salted dried fish, while the entire floor was taken up by a stained coir mattress. As they approached, the smell hit Bella like the Blind Watchman's hand, and her gorge rose. Disagree did not pause, ducking inside. Bella took a deep breath before following, her stomach heaving every time she was forced to inhale.

They found the Blind Watchman's cache buried inside the mattress—knives and swords, guns, clothing, and jewelry. To her delight, Bella found both her switchblade and her medallion at the top of the pile. In addition, she armed herself with a brace of pistols, a bag of fireballs, and a coil of sturdy rope.

After finding and discarding several items, Disagree changed his soiled pantaloons for another, slightly tighter pair with red stripes. He chose a machete whose blade he tested on his thumb, as well as a wide-brimmed straw hat. Noting the wisdom of that last choice, Bella also found a hat—an old-fashioned tri-corner that fit her nicely. Then she followed Disagree in filling her arms with dried fish. Grateful to escape the stench of the cave, they returned to the beach.

The tide was falling, and the Blind Watchman was now lodged among the rocks. Crato was nowhere to be seen. *So much for caring*, she thought. *He probably stuck around just for the handouts.*

Disagree spoke directly to her thoughts. "He probably goes to warn them. They know you come now."

"I'll take my chances," she replied.

They launched their boats in silence. Bella felt satisfied at how her dugout handled under sail. Though torn through in several places, the canvas caught and held the wind, swiftly driving the knife-like hull through the clear green water. In the past weeks the wind had set out of the southwest, and it would stay there for months to come. With luck and barring a squall, she could run the dugout all the way to The Elder's Island.

She looked back. Disagree had set his sail to a close reach, the skiff slipping away at almost a right angle to her while he regarded her over his shoulder, sad in the way that only a stone can seem sad.

Perhaps he won't say anything, she thought, and suddenly, she felt bereft.

Disagree called, "Not just you have secrets. With this or without this, you are a great treasure to him."

Bella frowned. "What do you mean?"

"I keep my secrets too," Disagree replied. "You can find out in time."

He turned to watch the horizon ahead. The gap between them widened. Bella had the urge to turn the dugout, but she resisted. *It's his last ruse*, she thought. *Try a bribe when all else fails.*

"I suppose I will," she called. "Goodbye, Dis."

Disagree kept on sailing. His silence hurt her, but not enough. She turned her attention to her boat, now watching the pontoon cutting white lines in the water, now turning her eyes to the triangle of the lateen sail, as the monsoon drove her on toward the East in a single, endless breath.

Chapter Ten

Like the shadow of a mountain, Disagree emerged from the trees. The king's house was lit up on all sides by oil lamps hanging from the eaves. Clouds of insects circled the lamps, some throwing themselves at the glass, sizzling as they hit. The sentries' hands went for their rifles, then relaxed when they saw Disagree. One gestured at the back door with his head.

"He's taking care of someone in the basement. He said come down if you want, or wait in the kitchen."

Disagree grimaced. He had seen too much of what the king did in the basement to have any interest in it. Hodoul must have known how he felt, to give him the option of staying in the kitchen.

Only the dim after-image of the veranda lamps relieved the darkness of the back corridor. Disagree paused to glance into the room where the king slept and noticed the coir mattress dragged to one side. A faint square line of light betrayed the trapdoor set into the floor. From below, a faint rhythmic *thwup* rose up. That and nothing else. He grimaced again. *Nearly done with him.*

Disagree slipped into the kitchen and sat at the far corner of the table. He thought about Bella—how she was making out—and the poor wretch hanging in the basement. The last two times the king had administered his law, the prisoners had almost died. That silence did not bode well.

A few minutes later, he heard footsteps rising from below in the next room. The back door swung open.

"Get him out," came the rasp of Hodoul's voice. "And make sure he lives to tell what happens to deserters."

Hodoul strode into the kitchen a moment later, carrying a long heavy cane with bumps along its length. He glanced in Disagree's direction but did not acknowledge him. Dis knew better than to think that Hodoul had not seen him. *Perhaps he is angry I did not come down.* Going to the sink, Hodoul ran some water over the cane, running one hand slowly up and down the shaft. Then he turned off the faucet and left the cane to dry on the edge of the sink. He came over and lit a lamp hanging over the kitchen table. The light flared and flickered, and the first thing Disagree noticed was the spots of blood that dotted the king's white shirt.

"Don't start with me," the king said. "I don't have the luxury of your mercy." Hearing something in Hodoul's voice, Disagree raised his eyes to that angular, ruined faced with its mountain of silver curls. In the grey eyes, dead to anyone else, he recognized a faint but definite anxiety.

He is not angry, just worried about Bella.

"Where is she?" the king said.

"She will not come back. She says she have something to do for you."

The expression on the king's face did not change, but there was a faint easing of tension in his body.

"And the Blind Watchman?"

"Dead."

The king was silent. "So where did she go?"

Disagree looked at him. "She go on. She says, something she must do for you."

Hodoul smiled. "I suppose you want to know what it is."

Disagree said nothing.

"I need to test her," the king said. "I need to see. Those men will eat her alive if she is not ready. You know the things I have to do." He looked toward the corridor. "Would she do them?"

"Perhaps she does not need to do them."

The king's eyes narrowed. "What are you saying?"

"Perhaps you can leave her alone—"

"Never," Hodoul hissed. "I will not go down to dust! Not after all this!"

Disagree knew better than to pursue this particular point.

"And you will respect my plans," Hodoul continued, his eyes baleful.

"Of course, Majesty," Disagree murmured. "Always—you know."

The king's eyes softened.

"Yes," he said. "I know. But you seem to forget yourself sometimes."

"That little one. She makes me forget."

"I can't afford that," Hodoul said. "I suppose that is why I am king. Now, we have work to do. I want you to go and parlay with the Princes. Apprise them of the Blind Watchman situation and propose a combined raid. We all meet at the monster's island and sail on to the East, portions to be assigned according to our agreed treaties. All right?"

"What about the Overlords? They do not want—"

"The Djinn be damned," Hodoul snapped. "I won't be treated like some underling minding their sheep. I am Jack Hodoul. I would rather kick at the end of a rope than dance on the end of their strings. They will learn to respect me!"

Disagree inclined his head. "So, you want me to go now?"

"Yes, now. Are you tired?"

"I sleep a little already."

Hodoul put his hand on Disagree's shoulder. "Rest a little in my room if you want, then go. Sail with the tide."

Chapter Eleven

Day after day, the waves followed her in procession. Each one swept forward to tilt the dugout down its face, the bow throwing up wedges of foam before the crest slid amidships and the boat came level. Then the wave surged ahead, and the dugout tossed back, the sail collapsing, then snapping full as the next wave came forward and the wind drove her onward again.

Bella sweltered through the mornings under the shade of the lateen, with her tri-cornered hat pulled over her face. The worst came at noon, when all shade vanished and the sun beat overhead. Some days clouds sailed up from the horizon and piled into thunderheads before unleashing a rainstorm. Then Bella put out empty coconut shells to collect water, and having satisfied herself that only the fish could see her, she bathed, spreading her clothes under the downpour.

The rain let up, as if someone had stopped working a pump. Bella beat some of the water out of her clothes and dressed, sighing at the coolness on her skin. A shell brimming with rainwater was a welcome relief from coconut milk, and still sipping, she settled with her feet in the warm ocean to watch the sun exploding into colors on the horizon behind her.

At those times, Bella thought about Dis. They had often watched the sunset, eating the sweet meat of the jackfruit and competing to see who could spit the seeds the furthest. She missed his presence now and kept glancing around, overcome by an inexplicable sense of imbalance.

Dis had been the first person she had met among the Brethren. In those first foggy days after she came from the Tree, he nursed her back to health in his own bed and made her drink strong, sweet tea, the taste of which she now recalled with a hateful fondness. He fed her plates of roasted breadfruit and grilled tuna, doing everything in a silence she found disconcerting at first but learned to love. She could still remember his first words, spoken with an expression so certain it might have been carved in granite since the beginning of time—"You come to a sad place."

The king visited her bedside—she did not find out until later what a remarkable boon this was. He stood looking down at her with his riot of hair, his broken features, and his calm, dead eyes, and her first thought was that somehow she should know his name.

"She isn't fat enough," he said, looking at her but speaking to Disagree. "Perhaps a few sweets, some nougat."

"I don't know how," Disagree replied.

The king turned his head toward him, eyebrows raised.

"My Mama always make it for me," Disagree said in self-defense.

"Then get Bessie, down the road, to make some. Feed her up. I don't want anyone to think I starved this one."

In the following months, she often wondered why he had chosen to favor her when he ignored all the other "new fish." She had found no satisfactory explanation until the night he proposed her mission. And then he had sent Dis to help her escape from the Blind Watchman. *Why? It must have been because of what Dis said, "You are a great treasure to him."*

Every day, she replayed the same sequence of memories until she came to an inescapable conclusion: the king must have chosen her from the beginning. After all, it stood to reason. Everyone said the king had sold his soul to gain Djinn powers. Perhaps he had the power to foretell the future... *Rise to the heights*, he had said. And the more she thought about it, the hotter the icy flame burned within her. Perhaps she would be the first queen of the Brethren, no longer wandering among the shacks of the camp, watching the lights in the windows and listening to the families inside. She would sleep in her own house. When she was present they would have to bow and call her, "Your Majesty," and they would listen when she spoke.

After the sun went down, the nights came over without warning. Stars pricked through in clusters. Bella traced the constellations with her finger: the Phoenix and the Crown, the Table Mountain, the Hare. Still thinking, she rearranged herself lengthwise in the hull, her head propped on a coconut just beneath the helm. The motion of the dugout and the heavy *whup-whup* of the lateen lulled her toward a sleep she knew would never quite come.

Oh, for some Claw, she thought. Then, *It's been a while since I thought about it.*

By now, she should have been twitching like a hanging man, as she had often done when the supply dried up. But, confronted by her new sense of purpose, her addiction uttered a wistful sigh and retreated, leaving her with the serene conviction that nothing could assail her destiny.

After moonrise, a sound like a handful of pebbles hitting the water disturbed her. An arc of fish fluttered overhead on wings that glittered in the moonlight. One night, two of them misjudged their flight and dropped on top of her, knocking the wind out of her stomach and bruising her thigh. One flip-flopped, slipping out of her grasp before leaping back into the water. The other she finally beat to death with a club she had found in the bottom of the hull. She ate it raw, salted with seawater.

A string of islands appeared, marking her course—bulbous coral formations alternated with pillars and arches crowned with untidy vegetation. The waters turned pale blue and crystalline, and shoals of fish swarmed in the shallows, an explosion of color beneath her so thick she could dip her hand in and flip one out whenever she was hungry. When the water grew shallower still, Bella released the lateen, allowing it to flap in the wind, while she stepped out knee-deep and waded up to explore the islands. But none of them grew fruit trees, and Bella sailed on, wondering how long the remaining supplies of coconuts would last.

A week later, she saw a cloud of terns wheeling and diving over a dark mound on the ocean, and her spirits rose. Where there were terns, there had to be water and perhaps some fruit. As she sailed in toward the island, the terns grew thicker, darting around so rapidly she thought it was a miracle they did not collide. They rose from the surface of the island, spiraling up into a cloud about fifty feet above. Others descended from the cloud to fight for space among the hundreds of grey shrieking bodies nesting on top of one another, so dense the ground writhed and fluttered, as if the earth itself were made of terns.

Bella searched in vain for a change in the color of the water. She was going to run up onto the rocks. She released the lateen in anticipation, and the boat slowed. As the dugout approached the edge of the island, she waited for the grinding sound of a collision. Instead a flock of terns broke into the air, and where a beach or a line of rocks should be, there was nothing but a loose tangle of twigs on the water. As she pushed on, terns rose in waves, revealing more water in place of land, until the whole flock rose up in a thunder of shrieks and flutters, raining droppings, loose twigs, leaves, and broken eggs. Bella found herself sitting in the midst of a mass of dead terns and branches that had formed a floating platform for the colony, which circled above, turning afternoon to dusk.

The dugout stopped. Confronted with the sea of bodies, a sudden sense of futility overcame her.

Perhaps I should just go back, she thought. *It would be all right, just like he said.*

Then she shook her head. *No. I won't go back to, "I told you so!"*

She pulled in the mainsheet and worked the dugout through the miniature sea of frail corpses and tangled vegetation. On the other side, she corrected her course by the setting sun.

The next morning, she woke to find the wind possessing a cool urgency. The ocean faded to a dull grey, breaking out with whitecaps. Clouds rolled overhead, not even a patch of brightness to betray the sun. The rain started, colder than the usual afternoon showers, the drops stinging her skin like stones. The wind rushed over the water, blowing foam off the whitecaps.

Then the storm was upon her. The world disintegrated into a tumult of wind and water. Within minutes, the dugout was swamped and laid over on its side. Bella clung to the hull as it whipped back and forth, and the water-drenched wind forced itself down her throat, up her nose, and into her eyes, blinding her with salt. The half-submerged hull battered her chest so hard that she wept at the pain, at one moment diving, at another tossing and spinning, defying her to hold on. The flesh on her hands softened, then tore and bled. Her nails ripped.

Minutes coalesced into hours. She felt her grip loosening. Just before she let go, she thought about Dis, and the sadness returned—the sadness she knew whenever the Claw began to take hold of her. A memory of the time before the Tree broke the surface of her mind. She had run away one night and now she could not go back. The sadness rose higher, covering her head like the waves. She wanted nothing but to let go. So she did, and the waves pulled her under.

For a moment, she resurfaced and saw a break in the clouds and a beam of light playing on the surface. *The storm must be over*, she thought. And she went under again. Water flooded her mouth and nose and burned in her throat. She choked, sinking faster with her legs and arms twitching.

And then she died.

Lethes II

Jonah Comfait sat on the rocks looking out over the ocean. The sun, newly risen, shattered on the surface. The monsoon breeze exhaled endlessly in his face. Jonah closed his eyes and took a deep breath before glancing at where the takamaka tree stood, like something ready to collapse.

I should do this, he thought. *It's getting late.*

The sense of futility overtook him again. After all, it wasn't as if he hadn't tried to help her. Perhaps it had been premature, but the last time he did so, just the week before, her reaction had scalded him—that vindictive, jeering expression, as if she had almost been looking forward to belittling him. "A magic lamp? Grow up!"

How long are you going to push this? he asked himself. Another part of him responded, *For as long as it takes!*

Jonah jumped to his feet and clambered up to the takamaka tree. He rolled away the small boulder that covered the opening and reached in, then snatched his hand back as something scuttled over it. A hermit crab wearing a tiny conch shell ran out and disappeared into a crevice in the rocks below. Jonah reached in again and pulled the Lamp from its hiding place. With both hands, he carried it to a flat spot and set it down.

He had seen it countless times, but every time he looked it exerted a new hold on him, as if it had recreated itself yet again. Nothing physical had changed, of course. It was still the same three-foot-high, minaret-shaped lamp that Captain Aquille, his old mentor, had presented to him—was it only two years ago now? The polished surface threw sunlight back in his face, forcing him to narrow his eyes to see the ornate grillwork pattern around the Lamp's core: fishermen on an ocean full of fish, Angeli fluttering above on their bodies of multiple wings.

As familiar as always, yet holding another depth he had never seen. What was it? He had struggled with the question of how ordinary things could get deeper. Then he recalled how Captain Aquille had struggled to learn the Lamp, and with what result? Nothing, until a dream had come to him and revealed the hidden meanings he had sought with such futility. In the end, Jonah thought, perhaps he could never know the Lamp completely until it *wanted* to be known.

A movement at the corner of his eyes distracted him from his speculations. His mother was making her way among the rocks, leaping up onto a perch when a wave ran in before coming on toward him. She wore a blue floral dress today and had plaited her hair into intricate pigtails that wound around the back of her head. As Jonah watched her, all the disappointment and futility of the past two years reached a high point. If only she, at least...

He shoved the thought aside—he had been over it too many times—and forced himself to smile up at her.

"I thought I'd find you here," she said.

His mother sat beside him, tucking her skirt between her legs.

"Madame Morgan telephoned," she said.

"Oh?" he said. "Now what?"

"Isabella ran away again last night. Madame Morgan said she stabbed her father almost to death."

Jonah exhaled. He felt his shoulders sinking under an invisible weight.

"She was exaggerating, of course," his mother said, chuckling. "It was really no more than a deep scratch. He's just fine. I could hear him in the background, whining and complaining like a child."

"It's not the first time either," Jonah muttered. "He should be used to it by now."

"Is this worth continuing, you think?" his mother said. "Isabella doesn't seem to be making any progress, and I am sure your teacher wasn't expecting you to stick this long with the tutoring. If she doesn't graduate, she doesn't graduate. You can't achieve the impossible."

"I need to go," Jonah said. "She talks to me."

"She could talk to someone else," his mother pointed out.

"No, she can't."

"Why?"

Jonah was silent.

"Does your going there have something to do with this?" His mother gestured with her chin at the Angeli's Lamp.

Jonah shifted. "And if it does?"

"You want her to believe?"

Jonah looked at her. "Why not?" It sounded ridiculous, even to him.

His mother met his eyes. "You know you can't make it happen."

"I thought you of all people would understand," Jonah said. "You believed when I told you!"

His mother sighed and turned to look at the sea. "Yes. I believed what happened to you and your father. I believed it like I believed the dreams that told me you would both come home safely. But, Jonah—" She turned to him, her eyes begging. "As time went on, I realized there are other things more—" she struggled to find the words "—more, I don't know—"

"More important," Jonah said. He could hear the bitterness in his voice.

"No." She held up her forefinger. "Not that. Just things that needed to be secured in the meantime, if you know what I mean. And all of that was just more urgent than Mysterion, as wonderful as it is—" She broke off, seeing his expression, and sighed again. "I knew you wouldn't understand. You want everything on your schedule, and that's not how it works. You want Isabella to believe today and me to believe yesterday. And why? Not for us, Jonah. For yourself. You are doing this for yourself and no one else."

"What do you mean?" Jonah felt his face getting hot.

"You think that if someone—anyone—believes, you won't feel as if you've failed. The truth is, you are not using the Lamp to help others to rediscover Mysterion, but so you can feel worthy."

She stood up, dusting the back of her skirt. She looked down at him.

"You chose truth when you chose the Lamp," she said. "I just spoke the truth. Take it as you wish."

Jonah said nothing.

"I will have lunch waiting, either way," she said.

"I may not be back," Jonah muttered.

"Then I can warm it for dinner."

She picked her way down to the beach, leaping among the rocks like a little girl. Jonah watched her. He wanted to be angry—felt angry—but another side of him realized she was right. After all, what was that impulsive attempt to speak about the Lamp with Isabella, except desperation?

Looking at the Lamp, he thought, *Why even bother?* His other voice answered, *Because you were given this task.*

Taking a deep breath in, Jonah picked up the Lamp. It felt heavier than ever as he rested it on his knees. With a sense of doing what he had done so many times before, he blew gently into the Lamp's core.

Chapter Twelve

So, it's true—death doesn't stop your thoughts. How disappointing. Then Bella became conscious of moving through water. She lay, facing downward, her arms pressed to her sides and legs together, like a submarine sarcophagus flying through the darkness.

Are you Isabella Morgan?

A woman's voice had spoken into her head. Fighting whatever bound her limbs, struggling to control the chaos of her heartbeats, Bella tried to reply. No sound emerged. Water flowed easily into her throat and lungs, and she knew she was not breathing air.

Am I really dead? she thought.

The response came. *We decide that. Are you Isabella Morgan?*

The voice—cheerful and matter-of-fact—belonged to a young woman. Bella thrashed and shook her head.

That's not my name.

Anymore, you mean.

What?

It's not your name anymore.

Bella twisted her head around in terror. The darkness pressed into her vision, and the voice continued. *My mother gave me my name. It reminds me of her—Cybele, she always said, swim close to me, it's dangerous.*

Where are you?

I am close.

I can't see you, Bella said.

It's night. But if you look from where we came, you can see our wake.

Bella twisted her head over her shoulder and saw phosphorescent streams spiraling away from her.

The voice resounded in her head again. *Is that why you don't want that name?*

I don't understand, Bella said. *Who are you?*

Because you don't want to remember that they gave it to you?

Am I dead?

We decide that.

When? Where are we going?

No fretting about it. You will see when we arrive.

I can't move!

No, you can't. We bound you for the journey.

Where? Bella screamed inside her head. *Where are we going?*

Shh. Calm yourself, my love.

Bella struggled and contorted in fury, but her limbs stuck fast. She opened her mouth and screamed with all her strength. The sound resonated in her imagination. At last she subsided, her lungs heaving in slow motion. This must be her captor's magic. She wasn't dead, just bewitched.

With a great effort, she regained control of herself and forced her limbs to relax. After a minute of concentration with her eyes closed, her breaths slowed. Her mind acquired an unnatural calm. *If she asked me about that name, she was expecting me... How did they know? But that doesn't matter, stupid. Just like Dis said, Crato must have warned them and they were waiting. But not to kill me. As a prisoner, I'm more valuable...*

She opened her eyes and spoke a thought. *My name is Isabella Morgan.*

Good. Isabella could almost hear the person smile. *I knew it somehow.*

How did you know?

I don't know... The voice sounded vague. *Perhaps you just look like it.*

Are you joking? Bella thought. *And how's an Isabella supposed to look?*

Not an ordinary Isabella. Just a pirate one.

Oh, I see. Bella felt her fury rising. *And how's a pirate Isabella supposed to look?*

Thin as a stray cat. Tangled hair. Just like you.

You know lots of pirates named Isabella who look like that?

Not really. Just you.

So, you knew I was Isabella because you knew what I looked like.

Perhaps. The Elder showed you in our Seeing Pool.

And how did he know me? Bella said.

He didn't say.

So I'm not going to die, then.

The voice was smiling again. *We're all going to die, my dear. At least until the Higher Mysterion comes.*

Now, I mean!

Well, you're not dead now, no.

Bella gritted her teeth in frustration. *I mean, you don't want to kill me.*

Oh dear, no. We don't do that.

So what do you do?

We bring back the dead. Or we leave them as they are.

So you brought me back. Where are you taking me? To this Elder person?

You'll see, my love. A hand stroked Bella's cheek. She jerked away.

Poor thing, the voice said. *You aren't used to that, are you?*

Leave me alone. Just tell me where you're taking me!

As I said, the voice murmured, *you will see. Until then, why don't you just enjoy the journey, hmm?*

A Djinn's fart on that.

Well, then, perhaps we should talk again when you're a little happier.

Whatever you say.

The presence of the voice retreated from Bella's mind. The hole of silence amplified the beating of her heart.

The darkness was no longer a solid thing. Bella could tell distances within the void. The first light reached down and lit up tinges of green and blue. Then she saw them—a group of six mermaids gliding beside her. Three younger ones wore their hair arranged in elaborate spirals and giggled at one another in unspoken gossip. The two elders allowed their unbound hair to trail behind them and looked as if nothing could surprise them. Swimming closest was the mermaid Bella guessed was the leader, probably the one who had spoken in her mind—Cybele. She was older than Bella had imagined, with an ugly, pleasant face and hair plaited into two long ropes that trailed all the way down to her tail—that of a swordfish.

The mermaid looked down and met Bella's eyes. She smiled, but her presence did not enter Bella's mind, as it had earlier. That distancing bothered Bella, but she steeled herself to meet the mermaid's smile with unflinching defiance. The mermaid's smile grew ironic, as if she were aware of Bella's struggle, just before she turned her attention back to the course.

Only then did Bella realize that none of her escorts were holding her by a chain or a rope. She was simply floating between them, moving in exact coordination with their movements. She had been right, she realized—she was enchanted, and no amount of effort would be able to free her.

The light falling from the surface strengthened. Outlines of distant masses rose out of the green haze. As they swam closer, the shapes resolved into immense coral structures—towers and walls around which swarmed shoals of fish like underwater birds, rising, circling, and roosting.

They swept through coral mountains and over valleys. Then they broke out onto a great plain. Shipwrecks littered the sand as far as she could see. There were ships she knew—schooners and frigates and square-riggers and dhows—and others she could not recognize—odd, cylindrical shapes with round sails that looked as if they had been fashioned in an age yet to come.

The mermaids swerved through the maze of hulls and broken yards at a terrifying speed. They narrowly dodged the jagged edges and obstacles that rushed past, without a break in their tranquility.

Bella looked up at Cybele. *Where did the ships come from?*

Cybele smiled. *Calmed down a little, have we?*

Bella shrugged. *What choice do I have?*

That's the spirit, Cybele said. *The ships come from a great battle of*

Mysterion long ago.

Who fought? The Brethren?

No, this was before the Brethren. A battle between the People of the Wind and those who served the Djinn.

Who won? Bella said.

The Djinn, at first. Then the Elder rose up and defeated the Djinn.

But the Elder is gone now.

Cybele looked at her. *Yes.*

And Jonah is their leader now?

Cybele tilted her head. *Why do you ask about things you already know?*

Bella felt her face grow warm in spite of the cool water. They were past the ships now, sweeping over the open plain. It was bare here, except for patches of seaweed waving in the current and great shoals of angelfish and parrotfish moving in unison in the distance. Looking closer, Bella made out larger fish-shapes moving at the edges of the shoals. Were they sharks?

So why are you here? Cybele asked. *A one-girl pirate invasion from the West?*

Bella was silent. Perhaps it was best not to say anything.

I'm just teasing, Cybele went on. *I know this was a difficult thing to do.*

Bella felt relieved. *You're not making it any easier.*

I'm sorry, my love, Cybele said. *But we mermaids have a saying: Love a Djinn before you trust a pirate.*

I left the pirates.

Ah, but you see, that has yet to be seen.

Ahead, the shoals converged. The creatures she had thought were sharks were actually mermaids. Each held a net between two sticks as they drove the fish into a single swirling mass.

Bella decided to change the subject. *Catching a little dinner?* She gestured to the shoal with her chin.

They are not for us, Cybele replied. *We're taking them to the fishermen.*

A younger mermaid chimed in with a giggle, *And they think they do all the hard work.*

Cybele pointed. *Over there the shallows begin.*

Ahead, the plains ended and a flat-topped range of mountains spread across the ocean floor as far as Bella could see. The herders were driving the shoal forward now, following the same course as Bella and her escorts. At their speed, the distance between them shrank, looming higher until Bella could no longer see the tops. In some places, the cliffs jutted out, a maze of coral matted with seaweed and swarming with sea life. Then the walls receded into inlets whose depths were lost in darkness. The herders drove straight for the largest of these gaps.

Bella understood where they were going. *You're taking me to the People of the Wind.*

Patience, Cybele replied.

As they entered the inlet, darkness closed around Bella again, concealing her escort. They swam along in silence. Bella felt herself slowing until the water no longer flowed on her skin.

Where are we?

No answer. The silence pushed in on her. The presence of the mermaids around her had receded, and fear gripped her chest. In spite of the futility of it, she began to struggle against whatever bound her. To her surprise, her limbs came free from her sides.

The dark water began vibrating. Hundreds of currents beat against her skin. Bella froze, terrified.

What's happening? But even as she spoke, the words flowing past her lips turned to salt. Seawater raked her lungs. She clawed the water around her, kicking as the sensation of drowning overtook her.

A voice, Cybele's, spoke in her head with a new authority. *What do you want with us, Isabella Morgan?*

Bella shuddered but did not reply.

Tell me what you want!

Dying. Isabella choked out the word, her consciousness flickering.

You have been dead for years. Do you want to live?

Yes.

Then you have your life for now. Remember the gift and rise up!

In unison, the mermaids sang a hymn in the darkness. A strange wordless melody filled Bella's head, high and discordant with a drone in place of a harmony. A sudden rush of small bodies pressed against her, finning away from the mermaid's song, the press of them bearing her upwards.

Fish, she thought. She could see the surface now, ripples highlighted in the blue morning sky beyond. The narrow shapes of boats formed in a rough circle and heads peered over the gunwales.

She rose past the lower edge of the nets, buffeted in the storm of angelfish and bluefish and red snappers. She broke the surface in a crush of bodies that drove into her from every direction. Hands lifted her out as water spewed from her mouth and nose, and her breath flooded fire in her lungs.*even bother?* His other voice answered, *Because you were given this task.*

Taking a deep breath in, Jonah picked up the Lamp. It felt heavier than ever as he rested it on his knees. With a sense of doing what he had done so many times before, he blew gently into the Lamp's core.

Chapter Thirteen

When her coughing eased, she opened her eyes, only to narrow them against the sun. She lay on a bundle of nets at the bottom of a boat. Around and above, voices tumbled over one another.

"She's too thin, this one."

"Too thin, too fat. Is that all you think about, Magritte?"

"Uh, Dio, are you going to be giving out fish any time?"

"They should bring her to my house. I'd fatten her up with some nice nougat."

"They won't bring her to your place! If she goes anywhere, they'll take her to him, on the mountain."

"That red snapper there looks good. Dio, could you possibly...?"

"In a moment, Madame. Someone's gone to Jonah."

Jonah, Bella thought, and rolled her eyes upward. Several women stared down at her. Some had skin like new charcoal and green eyes, others had Asiatic eyes and skin the color of coffee with cream, and there were mulatto women with red hair and blue eyes. They all wore cotton dresses printed with lilies, orchids, and vines on sky-blue or sun-yellow backgrounds.

A black man with a heavy pleasant face bent over her.

"Well, hello there," he said, smiling. He spoke with a touch of a slur at the edge of his words.

"Michel, didn't I say to stay back?" Bella turned toward the voice—a pale man with sharp features.

Michel's face fell. "Sorry, Dio," he said. "I just wanted to say hello."

"*Love a Djinn before you trust a pirate*. While you're saying hello, she could stick a knife between your ribs."

"Oh," Michel said. He looked down at Bella. "She doesn't look dangerous. She looks lost, that's all."

Bella's hackles rose. She tried to rise. Her muscles screamed and she sank down. Whatever magic the mermaids had used to bind her had also served to numb her body. Now she remembered the wounds from the storm—the bruises on her chest and her fingernails torn to the quick.

Michel had backed away at her movement.

"Just leave her, I tell you!"

"All right, Dio." Michel sat beside Dio on the gunwale.

"Don't move, Miss," Dio warned Bella. "You're not going anywhere anyway without a guard."

Bella spoke through her pain. "I thought the People of the Wind were supposed to be hospitable... to strangers."

"Hospitable, yes. Not a bunch of fools."

"So, I'm a prisoner then."

"Not exactly," Dio grinned. "You can't trust anyone these days. Let's just say you're on probation."

Silence fell as the people stared at Bella. Dio had inspired them—she could see a new fear in their eyes.

Something occurred to her. She reached up to her throat. At first, she could not feel the cord and panicked. Then—there it was. She slipped the doubloon back into place.

Dio grinned. "What you were looking for, *Miss*?"

Bella said nothing.

"Don't worry," Dio said. "We didn't touch your little necklace."

"I know," Bella croaked. "You'd be missing some fingers if you did."

Dio grinned wider and opened his mouth to reply.

"There they are," one of the women said.

The others turned. Bella dared not move.

Dio addressed someone outside her line of sight. "Found her in the nets this morning."

A head appeared over the edge of the gunwale. He was a boy her age, perhaps a little older. He had dark skin and sharp, carved features. His black eyes glittered like lumps of washed coal.

"You are calling yourself..." The boy's accent reminded Bella of Apoojamy, but not as pronounced.

"Bella Couteau," she replied, meeting his eyes.

"And the name you left in the Tree?"

He knows about the leaving of names. He was one of us!

"Isabella Morgan," she said.

The boy glanced behind him and nodded to someone out of Bella's sight.

"It's her," he said.

They know! It's over.

The boy turned back. "I am Sartish," he said.

Hodoul's ward, Bella thought. *The one who ran away!*

"I... I thought you died," she said.

Sartish smiled—a sharp, lopsided grin. "That is the story they relate. Are you capable of getting up unaided?"

Bella tried to push herself upright again and gasped.

"Are you requiring some assistance?" Sartish said.

"No," Bella grunted, and tried again.

Sartish glanced behind him again and gestured. "Azrel, provide her assistance."

"I'm fine," Bella insisted. Her eyes had filled with tears at the pain.

"You are wasting time," Sartish replied. Then the Azrel he had addressed appeared, and Bella fell back, overcome by the vision of the creature who rose above her against the sky. From the descriptions of those who had seen one, she recognized an Angelus—*a creature of wings and light*, they said. She had not believed them. And yet, here it was. Long wings entwined to formed the semblance of limbs. Tiny wings nestled around a body. Wings blew around its head like locks of hair. And always light fluttering everywhere. Only the Angelus's face was flesh—a full heart shape, with a sarcastic mouth and bright green eyes mocking Bella.

"It's my lot in life," Azrel remarked. "Carrying humans who can't seem to stand on their own two feet."

"I can stand just fine," Bella replied. She began struggling again.

"Unlikely," Sartish said. "Take her, Azrel. The Elder is waiting for us."

"Then she needs to hold still and let me do it," Azrel snapped.

"Cease your struggling," Sartish said to Bella. "At once."

Bella ignored them both and pushed herself further upright as the pain threatened to black out her vision.

Sartish grabbed her throat. "Desist." Bella choked, fumbled, trying to break his grip, but his hand seemed to have been carved onto her neck. She noticed that his forearms were covered with small pockmarks. Still struggling, she reached down to where she had hidden her switchblade. It was gone.

"This is what you're looking for?" Dio displayed the blade in his hands.

"First thing we take," Sartish grinned at her. "I know how it works."

"Let go," she gasped.

"Stop then."

Bella relaxed her struggles. Sartish let go. As Bella doubled over, coughing to regain her breathing, Azrel pulled her up onto her back. Bella squirmed, disturbed by the sensation that she had fallen into a nest of birds. Azrel rose above the crowd. In either direction the beach stretched, white and blinding, until it curved out of sight. Green waves rolled off the open ocean. With Sartish following, Azrel floated toward the head of the beach where the island rose up in a wall of coconut and mangrove trees. The crowd watched their progress, then turned back to the forgotten catch, haggling over who would get what, with Dio acting as mediator.

"Joe would love a nice red snapper for dinner, cooked with chilies."

"If it's not too much trouble, I'll take that tuna. That one there."

"But he's only one man. I have five children to feed!"

"Would you please make up your minds. Some of us have things to do!"

"Dio, you decide."

"Well," Dio began portentously. "In my opinion…"

But the rest of Dio's opinion was lost as the beach fell behind Azrel and Bella and the trees closed around them. No longer stirred by the onshore breeze, the air thickened to the consistency of heated oil. In the branches, myna birds squabbled over ripe jackfruit with shrieks that intensified the heat. Azrel floated above a narrow, beaten path between the trees. Bella wondered where Sartish had gotten to…

His voice came, irritated and distant behind them. "Slower, Azrel!"

Azrel sighed and slowed to a hover. "It seems a miracle to me," she said, "that human beings have intelligence enough to stand on two feet. How do you manage it? It must be like walking on stilts! A bit challenging for creatures of your level of intellectual development, if you ask me—"

"Didn't ask you," Sartish said, coming up beside them. His hair glistened and his dark face ran with sweat. "But I will be informing you of this much: the Wind made a mistake giving you a mouth."

"Well," Azrel replied, raising her eyebrows. "If you won't listen to the ageless wisdom of the Angeli—"

"Not that I will not—I'm having no choice, that's all."

Azrel's smile took a provocative turn. "You can always go back to the pirates."

Sartish inclined his head. "Sometimes you make me think about it. So much for the wisdom of the Angeli."

Azrel struck her breast. "Ah, Sartish, you wound me! You don't really mean that, do you?"

"Want to test it?"

"Fine, Mister I-think-I-know-better-because-I've-seen-both-sides. Lead the way."

Sartish inclined his head. "At last, some true wisdom!" He grinned at Bella and then strode on. Azrel followed, and Bella heard her mutter things like, "Look at that—he just set a new record for all-time slowest land speed by a bipedal creature," and, "If we were going any slower we'd be walking backwards." Sartish didn't bother to reply, but he flashed a grin back at them to indicate that he had heard.

The path threaded its way up through the forest, jogging at odd angles. At length, it joined a red earth road lined with almond and breadfruit trees, beyond which the forest continued inland. Along the road strolled women in bright dresses and men in slacks, bare-chested or wearing loose shirts. A string of children wound by, engaged in some imaginary quest. They alone seemed to have a purpose. Everyone else displayed an irritating lack of urgency, walking several yards before pausing to sit and chat, then rising to move on or turning back where they came from.

As they joined the stream of traffic, several people called greetings to Sartish, who, in spite of his haste (and much to Azrel's annoyance), paused to say hello. Some of them regarded Bella with pointed interest, and Sartish explained, "A refugee caught in the nets."

Impressed nods. "Really! What's her name?"

Sartish glanced at Bella and grinned out of the corner of his mouth. "You can call her Isabella."

More nods and smiles. "Welcome, welcome."

Bella nodded without meeting anyone's eyes. She felt awkward and ridiculous clinging to Azrel's back, a feeling that did nothing to ease her general sense of frustration. She had hoped to approach the island and accomplish her mission, after careful observation and reconnaissance, with forethought and stealth. But even before she laid eyes on the place, she had been taken captive and stripped of her weapon. And now she was being carried along like an invalid in a pathetic procession, an object of curiosity for anyone with nothing better to do.

Sartish and Azrel moved on, forced to conform to the pace of the crowd. At last, the road entered an open circle of sand that reminded Bella of the parlay square back at home. At points along the circumference, groups of people emerged from the trees. They abandoned all pretense at direction and settled into little groups in the shade. The sounds of their conversations in the air were soft, desultory. Occasional laughter broke out like birdcalls.

Watching Sartish make the round of greetings, Bella could not restrain herself. "What are they talking about?"

Azrel shrugged under her hands. "Nothing, really. The air, the fish, the color of the sunset, their dreams."

"What's the point?"

"No point. Just an excuse to hear each other's voices."

"They all know each other then?"

"There aren't that many—a few hundred. My guess is they're all related by now!"

"Like one big, happy family," Bella said.

Azrel raised her eyebrows. "You don't like that?"

Bella smiled. "We're independent."

"You *were*."

"What?"

"You don't live that way anymore," Azrel said. "You live here with us now."

Bella shifted. Azrel's ceaseless fluttering was bothering her.

Azrel addressed Sartish. "Can we move along, Sartish?"

"Fine, fine," Sartish snapped. "Nothing wrong with being polite." He led the way at a fast pace, calling and waving his greetings as they went. Above the trees, a mountain rose like the fin of a great sea creature, running in either direction as far as Bella could see. Sartish did not pause at the forest but pushed on, finding a path among the fallen leaves and overgrown shrubs.

Another laughing, screaming line of children darted past and disappeared up the slope ahead. As Sartish, Azrel, and Bella followed, houses appeared. Small wooden bungalows with thatched roofs stood on carved stilts. Others were built around the trunks of trees, and still others were simple lean-tos with plank floors and walls made from billowing white curtains. Outside the houses, people sat in low chairs, sipping drinks and nibbling pieces of fruit. And again, the muted, languorous voices rose in welcome as they passed. This time, though, Sartish did not stop to talk. He was caught up in the effort of the climb through the morning heat, which had descended with full force. Further up the slope, the houses grew less frequent until the forest was a solid, unbroken wall around them. Even the sound of birds squabbling faded to a complete silence that filled every space in Bella's hearing.

Yet another group of children rushed by them. Bella frowned.

"Where are they going?" she asked.

"Same place we are," Sartish grunted. He did not elaborate.

Several minutes later, the forest thinned and gave way to knee-high scrub and then to a granite plateau carpeted with moss and lichen. Once they were clear of the trees, the wind buffeted Azrel as she followed Sartish. The narrow path wound its way to the mountain peak in a nest of bright, tumbling clouds. The children vanished, but this time Bella kept hold of her curiosity.

While Azrel sighed and muttered, Sartish paused here and wiped his dripping forehead. Bella looked back. The canopy spread below, while in the distance, the ocean was an expanse of shattered reflections that darkened in patches as great, solitary clouds sailed above.

Sartish had pulled out a clear flask and took a long drink. He offered the flask to Bella. Thirst won out over her hesitation, and she took it without a word. The liquid was water, as fresh as citrus and surprisingly cool, as if it had just been taken from an underground stream. She drank her fill and was surprised to find that the flask was no emptier than before.

"It was coming from above the heavens," Sartish explained.

"But why doesn't the water go down?" Bella asked, her curiosity forcing her.

"Don't know," Sartish said. "But I am certain it is not water. It is what our water comes from, or something."

Azrel sighed. "I've explained this to you *ad nauseam*, I think."

"Nausea is correct," Sartish muttered.

"Then perhaps you should listen for once," Azrel told him. "It is the *ideal* form of water," she explained to Bella. "It comes from the stream of Okean, and unlike water, it can never be consumed."

The stream of Okay-an... Bella was puzzled, but she resisted the urge to ask. Her survival now depended on silence. How much did these people know about why she was really here? It might well be everything. Crato might or might not have told them about the Blind Watchman's death. Either way, if they succeeded in drawing her into conversation, they might lead her into further betrayals.

"Feel any better?" Azrel asked.

Bella realized her body no longer hurt. She flexed her limbs. *Good as new!* she thought. *I must get some of that water.*

"Can you walk?"

Bella nodded, glad to get out of her ridiculous position.

"Good." With relief, Azrel dropped her to the ground. "But I will ask you to walk ahead of me, please."

"So I *am* your prisoner," Bella said.

Azrel shrugged. "If that's how you want to think about it."

They continued up the mountain. Bella's muscles warmed, and she kept pace with Sartish even on the steepest parts of the path, while Azrel floated behind them. The wind pushed and moaned from below, cooling the sweat on Bella's back.

Then, almost without warning, they stepped up into the cloud. The panorama of the island and the ocean was blotted out. A brilliant space opened up, where sunlight and wind mingled into bright banks and spirals and trails that gathered and circled endlessly. The air was cooler here, a relief from the solid heat below.

Sartish strode on ahead, unerring in his direction. Bella knew the peak must be close, but the cloud concealed everything, including the path beneath her feet. For all she knew, she could be walking on the edge of a cliff. One misstep and... The thought brought her to a halt.

Her stomach fluttering, she looked for Azrel—the Angelus was almost invisible, white on the white of the cloud.

"Where are we going?" she called.

"Just follow," Azrel replied in a muted voice. "Sartish knows where to go."

"How do I know that?"

Sartish's voice floated back to her. "Getting too far behind me, and you just might be taking the quick way down."

"He's right," Azrel advised. "You can't afford not to trust him. Keep moving."

Bella gritted her teeth and strode to catch up with Sartish with as much speed as her fear of stumbling would allow.

After some time, Sartish spoke again. "We're here."

Bella looked at the swirling bank of cloud around her and opened her mouth to ask him where "here" was, when Sartish vanished. She stopped, hesitant, and fear overtook her again. "Go on!" Azrel's voice commanded, almost in her ear. Bella took a few steps and, as if she had walked through a door, the cloud fell abruptly behind her. She was standing in naked sunlight again.

An expanse of carpet grass spread before her. And here were the children, running back and forth, shrieking with laughter. Farther away stood a bamboo gazebo roofed with coconut thatch. In the distance, horse-like creatures grazed at the edge of a forest, while leaves swirled above.

The noise of the children focused her attention. They were crowded most thickly at the center of the field. Bella wondered what was going on when a single child rose above the others, bucked around a few times as if riding a very small horse, then rolled off and out of sight.

Sartish glanced back at Azrel. He looked both amused and exasperated.

"At it again," he said.

The children parted before them, staring up at them in wonderment. But even the sight of Azrel failed to distract them for long. They grew more and more reluctant to make way. Sartish had to push the last few children gently aside to reveal the sight that had captivated them.

A young man—he looked about seventeen years old—ran around on his hands and knees, bucking and rolling his eyes in a faithful imitation of a wild horse. At his every movement, the children emitted screams of laughter. When one tried to get on, he paused just long enough for the child to get settled, then reared up to toss them off, snorting with amusement.

Sartish sighed. "Your Highness."

Bella was incredulous. *This... ?*

The young man looked up, shook his head as if whipping around a mane, and bucked around some more. Then he glanced beyond Sartish, noticed Bella, and after circling at a trot, rose to his feet.

"Enough for today!" he cried.

A chorus of disappointment rose up. "More horsey, please, please, please!"

"No," he said firmly. "I have to do some grown-up things now. Off you go!"

More pleas.

"Off you go!" he commanded.

Slightly subdued, the children trickled away toward the cloud bank. A few resilient stragglers remained, still begging for more horsey, until the young man had to wave them away with both hands.

"There's just no pleasing them," he laughed, as the last remnant scurried away. He had a round face, dark as coffee, but tinged with cream. He looked as if everything he saw were fascinating.

Either that, Bella thought, *or he's just soft in the head.*

Sartish bowed before the boy. "This is she, Your Highness. I am not certain she is wanting to be here."

The young man chuckled. "Most people live not wanting to be where they are, Sartish. And her name?"

"As you said, Your Highness."

"Isabella Morgan!" The young man clapped his hands and rushed forward to grab Bella's shoulders. Bella tried to shrug him off, but he gripped her tighter and caught her sullen, elusive eyes with his own. "Tell me, Isabella, do you believe in your dreams when they tell you things?"

"I don't know," Bella said, still trying to evade his gaze, but her heart beating faster at the sound of her full name.

"Well, I do." The young man's grin spread. "And lately, my dreams tell me that you have come to kill me."

Chapter Fourteen

Bella's heart broke loose, and a cold film spread over her skin. *They know! That damned parrot Crato...* It took all her resolve not to break Jonah's gaze and to keep her expression neutral.

"Believe what you want," she said.

Sartish gaped at Jonah. "May I inquire as to why you weren't informing us of this, Your Highness?"

Azrel sighed. "You know very well why, Sartish. His Highness wanted the girl to come without interference."

"And why would he be desiring that?" Sartish cried.

"I am right here, Sartish," Jonah said gently.

Sartish lowered his eyes. "Forgive me, Your Highness. I am simply bamboozled as to why you would let an *assassin*—" he glared at Bella "—within arm's reach of you at all!"

"Why not?" Jonah replied, shrugging. "Let her do what she has come to do."

Bella stared at him, nonplussed. *Is he insane?*

Sartish looked just as stunned. "Let her do..." he repeated. "Your Highness—"

"I trust that the Wind blows where it wills. Don't you?"

"Of course, but Highness, there's undoubtedly common sense also."

"Ah!" Jonah waved. "Overrated, in my opinion."

"So what, then," Sartish said, losing his patience again. "You are wanting me to give her the weapon she brought—" he reached into his pocket and pulled out Bella's switchblade. "You are wishing Azrel and me to leave you two alone so she can cut your throat in peace and quiet?"

"Something like that," Jonah smiled.

Sartish closed his eyes to get hold of himself. "I cannot be allowing this madness." He looked up at Azrel. "Up to now you won't shut up. Now you're mum. Say something, by the Wind!"

Azrel lifted her hands in resignation. "If His Highness says he is acting in trust of the Wind, what can I say?"

"You can say it is madness!" Sartish shouted.

Azrel shrugged and Jonah put his hand on Sartish's shoulder.

"Sartish," he said softly. "You must trust me. Give her the knife, and let me talk to her alone."

Sartish said nothing.

"Sartish, please. There is more in this than you and I know."

"I cannot." Sartish shook his head. "I cannot—"

"You can," Jonah said, and then, with steel in his voice, "and you will."

"It doesn't make sense!"

"It is the way of the Wind," Jonah said. "And it is my way. Unless you are reconsidering the choices you made..."

Sartish clenched his jaw and tossed the knife at Bella. Startled, she caught it.

"You kill him," Sartish told her, "and I kill you. Forget about any reward Hodoul offered. You'll be finished." He glanced up at Azrel. "Let's go," he said. Turning his back, he strode toward the cliff.

Azrel made a face—part apology, part exasperation—and muttered a sarcastic, "Yes, sir." Then she said to Jonah, "I will be listening for you. You need only whisper and I will be here." She glanced at Bella before bowing to Jonah and floating after Sartish.

When they were alone on the plateau, Jonah turned to Bella and smiled. "Are you hungry, Isabella?"

Bella was too overcome by the turn of events to reply.

"I'll bet you are," Jonah said. "Come, let's have lunch. Shantih probably put it out already."

He trotted away over the grass toward the gazebo, leaving Bella to follow at her own bewildered pace. When she arrived, he was seated at a low carved table with a steaming bowl before him.

He gestured at a place opposite. "Sit. Shantih!" He called back over his shoulder. An olive-skinned girl with a round, pleasant face emerged from the trees and skipped over to the gazebo.

"One for Isabella also, please," Jonah said.

Shantih stared at Bella with frank curiosity before skipping away for another bowl. She placed it in front of Bella, along with a spoon and a napkin, curtsied to Jonah, and scuttled away.

"She's the best cook I know," Jonah said, looking after the girl with admiration. "And only six years old!"

Bella looked down at her bowl and recognized clamsoup. Disagree had spoon-fed her this while she recovered from the Tree. She felt tears threaten to rise at the memory of his face looking down.

Jonah raised his bowl into the air. He held it up a moment, then lowered it and gestured to Bella.

"Try it. The best in Mysterion, as far as I know."

Bella's lip curled, but she did not remember the last time she had eaten anything and, in spite of herself, went at the soup until every last drop was drained. It was delicious, full of fresh ginger and garlic and made hearty by the rice. Still, it was not as good as the way Dis had made it.

"What do you think?" Jonah asked, leaning forward.

"Too much salt," Bella said.

He threw up his hands. "Everyone's a chef!" He went back to his bowl. When he had drained it, he sighed and sat back, staring out over the cliff at the ocean. The cloud had cleared, and Bella could once again see the heaving, glittering ocean spread to the horizon.

"I remember when I was a little boy," Jonah murmured. "We went to the south beach with our buckets. You couldn't swim there because there was no reef and the undertow was dangerous. The waves were huge and green, and they rolled down on the beach, *boom*—like that!

And we waited and waited until the waves washed out again, then we ran forward to find the clams. They're buried too deep to find, but when the water runs out they are exposed for a moment. Just for a moment, though, because they start digging right away and if you're not very attentive, they can be gone again, just like that. But if they were just getting under the sand, we always knew where they were…"

Because of the mark in the sand. Bella was not sure where the thought came from. She just knew it, that's all.

"Because they left a 'V' in the sand," Jonah went on, marking the air with his finger. "Then we dug as hard as we could and there it was! In the bucket it went with the others until it was time to go home and boil them up with onions and salt and a little garlic and ginger…"

He sighed and was silent.

"I know what you think," he said at last, looking at Bella. "You think I am a slave, and all these people," he gestured at the island below, "all of them are slaves too. You think of Mysterion as a place of liberty, and the Elder and his People a blot on the landscape, an offense to your freedoms. And the solution, in your mind, is to conquer or eradicate us. That is what they taught you, isn't it? When you came to them from the Tree?"

"I don't know," Bella replied in a surly voice.

"Well, I do, because that's what they taught Sartish."

"So, you're going to fix my mind like you did with him?"

Jonah smiled and shook his head. "Not at all. I'm just going to wait. You see, the little memory I recounted was not just nostalgic rambling. There was a point. In my experience, everything is revealed if you just wait long enough. And then, of course, you have to dig… But that too will come. Meanwhile, you can stay buried where you are. You may not want to discover the truth, but I promise it will discover *you*, sooner or later. It always does."

Just wait, Bella thought. *I'll show you the truth soon.* "And what's the truth?" she said out loud.

"The truth," he repeated. She waited for an answer, but none came.

Then, as she was about to speak again, he said, "Tell me, do you remember your life before the Djinn put you in the Tree?"

The question caught her off guard. "That's none of your business," she said.

"You do, don't you?"

"So what if I do? It's none—"

"Didn't you ever find it strange that you have a memory of your life as a Lethes?"

Bella said nothing. When she had come to the Brethren, she had made the mistake of asking a boy named Trent where he had come from before the Tree. The space where one of her molars had been still reminded her of his response. After that, she had learned to say nothing of the memories that swirled just beneath her consciousness, occasionally surfacing like the fins of frenzied sharks before diving again into the murkiness of her daily thoughts.

"You see, I think that's why you are here," Jonah said, raising one finger. "True pirates remember nothing. The Tree empties them of their memories. But not you. You remember."

A bruised cloud rolled up overhead, and now it began to rain—a sudden shower that drew a thundering grey curtain around the gazebo. A minute later, the storm passed. The cloud disentangled itself from the peak and floated on toward the ocean, trailing streamers of rain.

"What's your point?" Bella said. "That I'm not one of the Brethren because of a few memories?"

Jonah smiled and shrugged. "That's the little V-mark. It's up to you to find out what's buried."

"I'm not playing your little head games," Bella snapped. "First you give me a knife and say I can kill you, then you tell me I'm really one of your slaves. Forget it!" She stood and circled the gazebo before turning on him. "I should just cut your throat now and get it over with!"

Jonah laughed and clapped his hands. Bella flicked open her knife and strode forward, pressing it against his throat. "Do that again," she hissed, "and see how funny it is!"

He didn't even look at the knife. "Can I show you something first?"

"Why? So you can keep on with your little tricks? No thanks." She pressed the blade harder, and a trickle of blood ran down Jonah's throat. *Just one slash and it's done*, she thought.

"No tricks," Jonah said, wincing at the cut. "Just something that belongs to you, that's all."

Bella's eyes narrowed. "What is it?"

Jonah chuckled. "You will just have to wait and see."

Bella searched his face. She lowered the knife.

"Show me," she said. "And enjoy your last few minutes while you do it."

Jonah dabbed at the cut on his throat with the sleeve of his shirt and regarded the stain before smiling at Bella. "Follow me," he said, and walked out toward the forest. Bella stared after him, then closed and pocketed the knife. She followed him into the trees.

The ground was covered with pools that stretched as far as Bella could see. The path split into several branches, but Jonah did not hesitate. Passing each pool, Bella looked in and, below her dim reflection, saw a multitude of visions. In one, mermaids herded fish among the wrecks. In another, she saw a giant seagoing turtle, sunning itself on a sandbar.

Some sights puzzled her, like one that consisted of nothing more than flickering crystalline shapes. Others seemed familiar in an opaque way—a clock tower, where automobiles circled a roundabout; schoolgirls in striped uniforms skipping along a dusty path; an elderly man sitting on the step of his boutique.

"They are Seeing Pools," Jonah explained, forestalling her question.

"Some of those places don't look like Mysterion." She didn't tell him about her strange new curiosity.

"They see into the dreams of the Lethes—those we came from—both the past and the future. Ah, here it is."

Bella looked into the pool to which Jonah pointed. She saw an ancient-looking graveyard, lit by the early morning sun, and someone sitting in the shadows, leaning against a headstone. The vision was more than familiar—it stirred something in Bella, a fleeting sense of peace from another time.

"Who is that?" she asked.

She felt no real surprise when Jonah said, "That is Isabella Morgan."

"I liked to sit there," Bella said, before she could censor herself.

"You still do," Jonah murmured.

Bella frowned. "What?"

"What you are seeing now is the moment in your Lethes dream when you came here, and the moment you can return to."

"And this is what you wanted to show me?" Bella said, angry about exposing her feelings.

Jonah nodded. "I wanted to show you what you ran away from."

"Why? For what reason?"

"So you would know it is there. The truth is, you are still one of the Lethes, still asleep and dreaming. And you can return there, if you choose."

"Why would I want that?" Bella cried. "Have you ever considered that maybe it was a nightmare I wanted to wake up from?"

Jonah shook his head. "It would have been better to stay asleep among the Lethes than to embrace the illusion of the Djinn. Right now, you are just a copy of your true self, living the lie they sold you."

"What do you know about it?" Bella said in a strained voice.

"More than you think," Jonah murmured. "Look and see again."

Bella glanced again into the pool and started to see Jonah picking his way among the graves. He looked more careworn than the person by her side, but he was the same.

"You have known me before, Isabella," Jonah said.

In the pool's reflection, Jonah came up to where she sat against the headstone and squatted down. His lips moved.

Bella looked up at Jonah. "What is he—you—saying?"

"In his own words, he is saying the same thing I am saying to you now. Come with me, and I will show you a way to a new life. A chance to find your way back to Mysterion—" Jonah gestured around. "No escaping and lies this time. Only reality and life as it should be lived. With us, as one of the People of the Wind."

Bella felt a whirlwind of thoughts descending on her. She shook her head. "As one of your slaves, you mean."

Jonah shrugged. "You would have to submit to the Wind, as it has come to rest in me. You could call that a slavery of sorts, but—" he grinned "—it's better than being a real slave to that Hodoul."

Bella's face drained of its color. She stepped forward, pressing the knife hard against Jonah's chest.

"I am not a slave," she said.

"Your Highness!"

Bella and Jonah turned. Azrel was weaving among the trees with Sartish clinging to her back. The Angelus came to an abrupt stop before them, and Sartish leapt off, landing on the ground between the Pools. He bowed before Jonah before turning on Bella.

"Was she hurting you, Your Highness?" he said, a little out of breath.

"Of course not!" Jonah snapped. "I told you I would be fine. And I told you to leave us alone!" It was the first time Bella had seen him angry. The coldness in his voice surprised her.

"Forgive me. It was an urgent matter," Sartish said. "Otherwise Azrel would not be transporting me here."

"Too right," Azrel muttered. "It was an imposition as it was."

"And what was so urgent that you would disregard my express command?" Jonah demanded.

"The Brethren," Sartish said bitterly, pointing at Bella. "She led them to us."

Chapter Fifteen

Jonah, Sartish, and Bella stood at the edge of the plateau. Azrel floated behind them. The sun had descended almost level with their eyes, and the ocean glowed like heated brass. Seemingly embedded on the surface, the approaching armada swelled as they approached, their sails full in the wind.

"How in the name of everything did they get past the Blind Watchman?" Sartish said.

"He was probably dead," Jonah replied, glancing at Bella.

"You mean she killed him?" Sartish cried.

Jonah considered Bella. "I wouldn't be surprised."

Sartish's face turned grey. "He was our only defense," he whispered. "She killed us, too, then." He drew his dagger and advanced on Bella. She drew the switchblade and flicked it open.

"No, Sartish." Jonah moved between them.

"Even after this," Sartish demanded, "you let her live?"

"Yes," Jonah said, meeting his eyes. "I do."

"It is madness, Your Highness! Like putting your foot in your shoe when you are *knowing* there is a centipede!"

"She's not the centipede, Sartish. You of all people should know that. The centipede, if there is one, is down there." Jonah pointed down to where the ships had now anchored. The sails dropped, and men crowded the railings, readying skiffs to be lowered.

"Hodoul's coming, Sartish," Jonah said. "And I am not wasting any more time trying to stop you from doing what you *know* is not right. Are we speaking the same language, or not?"

Sartish's eyes flickered from Jonah's face to Bella and back.

"So, you're just going to leave her here?"

Jonah glanced back at Bella and smiled. "She can stay here if she wants, while we go down and guide the People back. At that time, she will have to decide where she belongs."

"You're not going to fight?" Sartish cried. "The Angeli can bring the swords…"

"For the Wind's sake, Sartish." Jonah rolled his eyes. "Are you going to argue everything I say? There is no purpose to fighting now. Do you not remember the history of Mysterion, what happened the last time we tried to fight those who were inspired by the Djinn?"

"That was different," Sartish said. "They had the Djinn with them."

"You know very well that the Djinn cannot fight with flesh and blood. No, the People fought their fellow human beings, and they were slaughtered, every one! There's no purpose in it, especially not when it comes to Hodoul. The best we can do now is form an enclave here, and then…"

"And then what?" Sartish said. "Wait to die?"

Jonah looked at him. "You are forgetting yourself."

Sartish lowered his eyes. "But it's suicide."

"I would never abandon the People," Jonah said. "When they are safe, we will take the next step. I know it is hard for you to understand, but the Wind is in everything that is happening."

Below, the skiffs launched from the ships—oars rose and fell in unison as they darted toward The Elder's Island.

Sartish watched them for a moment, then said, "Fine, let's go." He threw a final glare at Bella and began to scramble down the narrow path with dangerous haste, kicking stones off the edge.

"I sometimes wonder if he will ever come around." Azrel shook her head.

"Give him time," Jonah replied. He turned to Bella. "And what about you? Are you coming with us?"

Bella glanced down to where the skiffs approached and folded her arms. "And why should I help you?"

"Perhaps you shouldn't," Jonah replied. "Can I beg a ride down, dear Azrel?"

"You would leave her?" Azrel said, surprised.

"Not you, too!" Jonah threw up his hands.

"It's not that, Highness," Azrel said. "But supposing she were to try to escape—"

"She won't be going anywhere," he replied, climbing onto the Angelus's back but still regarding Bella. "She wants to belong somewhere, and her only two options are both now present on this island. Think about what I said, Bella," he said, as the Angelus floated off the edge of the plateau. "I will return with my People. You have until then to make a decision."

Bella watched the Angelus descend toward the tree line with Jonah on her back, her white brilliance answering the gold rays of the late afternoon sun. They disappeared into the forest, and Bella paced around as she chewed the nail of her thumb. Her insides were churning, and no matter how hard she tried, she could not bring her thoughts into order.

What will the king do? Would he kill her? Exile her again? The shame of her failure made her shudder. And then there was Jonah—what she had seen in the Seeing Pool, what he had said...

She shook her head and cried, "Coward!"

Her nervous footsteps turned her back to the edge of the plateau. The sun was low on the water. The skiffs had disappeared. She guessed they were beaching. From below, she could hear faint shouts, the continuous report of fire-rifles, an occasional scream. Then Azrel flashed out of the tree line below, floating upwards. Behind her trailed a ragged line of people—men carrying bundles of personal belongings and women carrying or dragging children behind.

As the head of the crowd wound its way up the slope, the tail emerged from the trees—the elderly, mostly, and a few who seemed to be wounded in some way. Jonah and Sartish followed last, encouraging stragglers who leaned on them for support on the difficult places. Jonah carried a child on his shoulders as he strode upward.

Is that all? Bella thought. She had somehow assumed the People would be more numerous than this. But here were no more than two hundred souls at the most, frailer and more pathetic than she had ever imagined. She understood why Jonah had refused to take up arms. The Brethren, at least ten times their number, would have eradicated them within hours.

An explosion lit up the trees. The crowd stopped to look back, and someone screamed. Sartish shouted and drove them forward. As the last of the stragglers started up the narrow path leading to the plateau, the first of the Brethren broke out of the trees, pausing to kneel and fire their rifles. Long flames lit up the sunset-flooded slopes. First one, then two and three people shrieked and collapsed. Azrel turned to gather up the wounded, carrying them up to the plateau in pairs. As she deposited the first inert bodies on the grass, she glanced at Bella.

"Comfortable, are you?"

"What am I supposed to do?" Bella retorted, aware of the horror churning inside her. "Have a good cry?"

Azrel made a disgusted sound and returned for more of the fallen as volleys of rifle fire broke out below.

The last of the People stumbled onto the plateau and collapsed, panting and weeping, staring around with shell-shocked expressions. Sartish and Jonah came last, supporting the oldest and weakest on their arms. Jonah lowered a little girl from his shoulder and pointed her to her family. He looked over at Bella.

"It's time," he called, gesturing.

With her heart beating, Bella picked her way through the subdued crowd to Jonah. Sartish watched her come, and she had never seen anyone look at her with so much hatred.

"They have captured or killed more than half of the People," Jonah said as she came to his side. "This," he gestured at the crowd spread out over the plateau, "is the remnant, and I won't allow any more of them to be harmed. You need to choose now, Isabella, whether you belong with me or with him." He turned and pointed down the slope. King Hodoul stood less than fifty yards away, by his shoulder the impassive bulk of Disagree. The sunset lit up the king's angular, crumbled features and glinted in his pile of silver curls as he stared up at Bella and Jonah. Behind him and Disagree the Brethren crowded, their numbers uncountable down to the trees.

"How are you doing, my dear Bella?" Hodoul called. "Sleeping well at night?"

Shock had turned Bella's skin to ice. She shivered in spite of the heat. Disagree shifted on his feet. Bella wanted to run forward to embrace him, but her feet would not allow her any movement.

Jonah was looking past Hodoul now—at Disagree, Bella realized.

"I've seen you before," he said. "You are Isabella's friend."

Bella started. *How does he know?*

Disagree said nothing, but Bella could feel his eyes reaching for her through the dusk. She stepped forward and opened her mouth. At that moment, Azrel appeared beside them, carrying a large, ornate lamp. As Bella wondered if that was really what she thought it might be, Jonah held the lamp high. The crowd on the plateau fell quiet, except for the whimper of a child and the moans of the wounded. Below, a restlessness swept through the Brethren like a wind.

"Do you see this, Hodoul?" Jonah said, his voice taking on a new resonance. "Do you know what it did?"

"I have no interest in your little toys," Hodoul's voice rattled up from below. He alone had not been disturbed by the appearance of the Lamp. His expression was as indifferent as ever.

"Then why don't you keep coming?" Jonah challenged.

"With pleasure," the pirate king replied. "Go on," he called over his shoulder.

The Brethren hesitated, looking at one another.

"If you value your worthless lives, go ahead!"

"I will go, Your Majesty!" a loud, arrogant voice cried.

Bella recognized the bald head and pigtail of Guillotine, her opponent in the king's challenge, pushing his way forward. He bowed before the king and then looked up and grinned. "No little hussy makes a fool of me and lives to remember it!" He ran at the slope.

As Guillotine approached, the Lamp brightened, as if fueled by the pirate's proximity. Guillotine ignored it, racing forward the last few yards with sweat running in rivulets down his face and bare chest. "Now you get what you deserve, you little traitor!" he shouted, drawing his sword.

A flame flashed from the Lamp. It arced outward to incinerate Guillotine before sinking back into a faint glow. Where the pirate had been, a cloud of ash hung in the evening air. Below, Hodoul looked pale. The Brethren moaned and stirred, and some retreated into the night.

Jonah leaned forward so that his voice would carry down the slope. "The Lamp will protect my People, Hodoul. If you try to come for them, its flame will consume you. You cannot win."

"We won't be leaving!" Hodoul shouted. "And you cannot stay holed up forever, you weak little man!"

"You are right," Jonah agreed. "So here is my proposal. You do not want my People. You want me."

Hodoul did not reply.

"At moonrise, I'll be sailing east to the Edge of Mysterion. I will leave the Lamp to protect my People. I will be unarmed. I challenge you to follow me! But only you and your ship. The rest of the armada must release their prisoners and return to the West."

Behind them, the People started spreading this new turn of events.

"You can't, Your Highness," Sartish hissed. "He'll hunt you down."

Jonah gestured to him to be silent. In the near darkness below, Hodoul's face was a pale sliver.

"Fine," the king's voice rose up. "They will go. And you had better run!"

Jonah turned to Bella and spoke in a low voice. "Do you remember what I said to you by the Seeing Pools?"

Bella did not reply. She felt as if she were encased in stone.

"Now you must choose," Jonah said. "Come with me and find out what I meant. Or go back down to him."

"Let her go!" Sartish urged.

"Bella," Jonah hissed, "decide!"

Bella squatted and buried her face in her folded arms. Something within her was tearing her apart.

"I can't," she cried. "I'm a traitor. He'll kill me!"

Jonah looked down at her. "Then you will come," he said. "And I will give you one last chance."

"One last chance to what?" Sartish cried. "Kill you?"

"Will you keep your voice down?" Jonah hissed. He leaned over the edge. "And one last thing, Hodoul. I will be taking your little traitor with me. I am sure she will prove helpful in anticipating any little tricks you may be planning. Try to keep that in mind, and save your energy!"

"I would be very disappointed in Bella if she did anything like that," Hodoul replied. "*Very* disappointed."

Bella knew the words were meant for her, and she shivered, still crouched down.

"Then you had better get used to being disappointed," Jonah said.

There was no response from below. Darkness had finally come.

"I think he is moving," Jonah said. "Azrel," he called softly. The Angelus, who had dimmed herself almost to darkness, fluttered forward. "Go and get Pierre." Azrel floated away and returned a few minutes later. From the corner of her eye, Bella saw an elderly man with charcoal skin and silver hair neatly combed and parted to one side. The old man knelt down.

"Rise, Pierre," Jonah said. "I have a task for you."

"The rumor is Your Highness is leaving," Pierre quavered.

"I am going East to lead the pirates away from the People."

Pierre made a visible effort to control his distress. "Will Your Highness return?"

"If the Wind blows this way, I will return."

"And the People? They are anxious about Your Highness."

"Take the Lamp." Jonah handed it to Pierre, who took it with shaking hands. "When the pirates leave, take the People down the mountain and guide them with my authority until I return."

"Your Majesty..." Pierre said, holding the Lamp as if it might shatter at any moment. "I am just a fisherman—"

"And I trust you better than anyone. I wish you to do this."

Pierre bowed again. "Very well, Your Majesty. Does Your Majesty wish to address the People now?"

"No. We must not draw attention to ourselves. The pirates will try to trap us before we can sail. Now, we must go," he said, embracing Pierre. No longer able to hold back his tears, the old man clung for a moment before bowing once more and backing into the night with the Lamp.

"Come, Isabella," Jonah said, leaning over where Bella squatted with her head buried in her arms.

"I don't want to!"

"You have no choice now. Either come, or make your way back to Hodoul and face what he has in store."

Bella looked up. "I hate you!"

Jonah smiled. "Don't shoot the messenger. Now, stand up."

With her jaw clenched in rage and her tangled hair hanging over her face, Bella got to her feet. As Jonah led the way, she followed with her feet moving automatically. Behind her came Sartish, his eyes burning into her back, while Azrel floated above them, offering just enough light for them to negotiate the clusters of people scattered over the plateau. They went quietly, assaulted by an occasional cry as someone recognized Jonah. But he did not stop, looking neither left nor right until they entered the forest.

They threaded their way among the Seeing Pools, sights now invisible in the darkness, until the trees gave way to another plateau. Bella realized that the forest bridged the two sides of the island. The eastern ocean glittered and heaved before them. A full moon was rising on the horizon.

"There she is." Jonah pointed. Bella lifted her eyes and squinted. Below them on the dark water, close in to shore, a sloop tossed against its anchor, as if it would set sail by itself if it could.

Jonah started forward. Sartish shoved Bella. "Move!" he snarled.

Bella spun round, her switchblade reflecting moonlight. Sartish's dagger rose and caught her blade with a sharp ring. They stood face to face, pressing and shifting to gain the advantage.

"Enough!" Jonah yelled.

"Good," Sartish whispered into Bella's face. "That's better!"

"By the Wind, Sartish, stop!"

"Tell her to stop, then!" Sartish shouted back.

"Isabella!"

"Tell him not to push me, or I'll cut out his guts!"

A hand gripped the back of her neck and jerked her backwards, out of Sartish's reach. She saw Jonah's face, hard under the moon. His hand grabbed her wrist and squeezed until she was forced to drop the switchblade. He left her to massage her wrist and strode over to Sartish.

"Give me the dagger!" he commanded.

"She drew on me!" Sartish protested.

"Give me the knife now, or you can stay here!"

Sartish scowled and looked down at his dagger. Above, Azrel watched in silence. For once, her face was grave.

"Fine," Jonah said. "You will stay."

"No, here it is," Sartish muttered, holding the blade out. Jonah took it and, in the same motion, tossed it over the edge of the plateau. "Now let's not waste any more time," he said.

"Aren't you going to take hers?" Sartish cried.

"Of course not," Jonah said, grinning at Bella, who had finally worked some feeling into her hand and was now massaging her bruised neck. "How else is she going to kill me?"

"You're mad," Sartish whispered.

"You just worked that out?" Azrel commented.

Jonah grinned up at the Angelus. "He's a slow learner. Yes, Sartish my friend, you are certainly right. I am mad by most standards. Nevertheless, there you go. You are stuck with this madman until the Wind changes its direction. Now, let's go. Bella, you follow Azrel. Sartish can take up the rear. I'm not letting you near each other for at least an hour."

After a terrifying descent down the mountain, in which Bella stumbled and fell several times, scraping and bruising her limbs, the ground leveled, and the vegetation gave way to a narrow stretch of white sand. There was no reef here. Giant waves, black and glistening, rolled unimpeded from the open water to explode on the shore, washing to within feet of the tree line.

Looking left and right, Azrel led them quickly to a small skiff tied above the high tide marker. Jonah and Sartish launched the boat while Bella watched them with arms folded.

As the skiff rode the first breaker, Jonah called to her, "Thanks for the assistance. Why don't you get in?"

Feeling as if someone had wound her up, some force now controlling her limbs, Bella waded knee-deep into the foaming water and climbed in. Sartish and Jonah ran the skiff at the next wave before leaping on board, each manning an oar just in time to take her over the crest and into the deep water. They worked their way out toward the sloop, whose movements seemed to grow more eager the closer they approached.

After they had docked, Jonah turned to Sartish and Bella. "I want to make one thing clear. From this point on, we work together. If Hodoul and his thugs get us, we're all dead—at least while I am still being allowed to live," he winked at Bella. "So, as much as you two are itching to get your hands on each other, it will just have to wait. All right?"

Sartish scowled. Bella hunched her shoulders.

"Good," Jonah nodded. "Glad to see you so agreeable. Now let's get ready to weigh anchor."

He looked at Bella. "I assume you are familiar with this?"

"Of course, I am!" Bella snapped.

"All right, all right," Jonah laughed. "Why don't you take foresails. Sartish on mains, and I'll helm."

Half an hour later, the moon reached its zenith in a sky thick with stars. *La Desirée* weighed anchor and slipped out of the lee of The Elder's Island under full sail. Azrel was a beacon, keeping watch at the masthead. Bella sulked at the bow and Sartish stood at the mainmast, while Jonah took the wheel, searching the horizon as he drove the eager little sloop toward the eastern Edge of Mysterion.

Only minutes after they left, *La Justice* rounded the north headland and set a course in the same direction.

Chapter Sixteen

Under full sail, they fled to the east. The empty ocean felt like infinity, and their days acquired a pattern that seemed to have existed for all time. Every morning they sat on the mid deck, eating fruit and drinking water-from-above-the-heavens as the ocean turned red and gold and lone clouds scudded across the sunrise. At last, Jonah rose. He spent the day at the wheel, guiding the sloop with eyes narrowed against the sun. Occasionally Bella would imagine he was asleep, only to see him make a slight adjustment to the helm.

For the most part, Bella manned the foresails, but Jonah had also made her responsible for swabbing the decks, polishing the cleats, and keeping the lines coiled when they were not in use. When she had sulked at the pointless vanity of these tasks, he had just grinned and winked. "If we're going to be cowards, we might as well be *organized* cowards."

She hated him more than ever when he said things like that.

At the masthead, Azrel spent most of the time glittering in a silence she broke at unexpected moments to drop pieces of sarcasm or irony on their heads. Then, without warning, she would be gone, only to return hours later with a single curt warning—"Two days," or, "A day and a half."

"What's she talking about?" Bella asked.

Jonah looked at her. "Your friends."

Catching a poisonous glance from Sartish, Bella went back to work with the sensation of being torn apart.

Sartish manned the mainmast until late each morning, when he pulled in the fishing lines that he had hung aft and chose a large red snapper or a tuna. He disappeared below to work in the galley, emerging several minutes later with a couple of full pans. He coaxed a wood-burning grill on the mid deck to life and brought the contents of the pans to a boil. They ate a lunch—usually a variation of fish and rice—in the merciless heat of the midday sun, sweating at the chilies Sartish was fond of adding to everything, trying to put out the fire in their mouths with deep drinks of water-from-above-the-heavens.

Sartish and Bella sweltered away each afternoon in what little shade the sails offered. They moved only to trim the sails, glad for the breeze that washed the deck in a steady stream. As the sun dropped down through the sky, they set to work again—Bella sulking her way through her cleaning tasks and Sartish going back down into the galley to prepare their evening meal.

They barely spoke to one another during those days. Bella could feel Sartish's hostility radiating at her whenever she approached, and more than once she turned to catch him staring at her. She tried to ignore him and went about her duties with renewed intensity, losing herself in frenetic activity.

She tried not to think about the reason she was here—the "second chance" Jonah had spoken of—but it came back to torment her throughout those days. She had not expected his cavalier attitude about his own death, the almost aggressive way he had offered himself to her. The challenge had proven to be the most difficult of her life—like a wall that rose up, insurmountable, as long as Jonah was willing to let her kill him. The situation enraged her, but she found herself helpless to do anything about it.

She spent her sleepless nights on the deck, while Azrel dozed in a dim light or flew away on her reconnaissance missions. The air was cool, and the wind blew steadily at her back while the stars littered the sky and the moon's reflection on the ocean dazzled her with the other side of noon. Sometimes, flying fish rose from the water and rained over *La Desirée* in a gleaming arc.

When her thoughts about Jonah lost their coherence, she thought of Disagree. She wondered how far behind *La Justice* was now, and whether Disagree was standing at the bow railing, wondering where she was. The sight of him standing behind the king in the half-darkness of the Elder's Island had evoked a pain that had not receded. And if she was to be honest with herself, she wanted nothing more than to sit with Disagree and eat plantains while the birds squabbled in the mango tree beside his shack. To rest in his silence again...

"Dis," she whispered to herself, and at once tears welled up within her. Then she clenched her jaw, angry at herself, and returned to the endless circle of schemes to provoke Jonah into a fight he would not survive, each more improbable, fanciful, and exhaustion-infected than the last.

Jonah seemed oblivious to her struggle. From the helm, he drew their attention to seabirds overhead, or clouds that he compared to this or that person—"Doesn't that one look just like Pierre when he is laughing?" At other times, he commented on the weather ("Looks like a storm heading north. Pity we missed it") or how delicious the food was ("I will never get tired of a good fish stew, Sartish!"). He never seemed to notice he was speaking in monologue, nor did he seem to see the growing tension between his two companions.

One afternoon, as they sat waiting for the noon heat to give way, Sartish swung on Bella.

"Do you know why I despise you?" he said.

Here it comes at last, Bella thought.

"Because I am one of the Brethren?" she said.

"No." Sartish shook his head. "I despise you because when I look at you, I am reminded of what I could become in a minute. Do you know—" he leaned forward "—that not a day goes by when I am not being tempted to do what you came to do? Do you not think I am tempted to be slitting his throat?" He gestured with his chin to where Jonah stood at the helm with his eyes closed. "And then I could be returning to the Brethren, to *him*, and he would have clemency on me and even be rewarding me. Do you not think I am considering this possibility every single day?" His voice was strained, urgent. "And when I regard you, it is by far worse yet. I want it more than ever. I want to do it, I want to kill him just like you..."

He broke off and looked away, trembling as he tried to get control. Bella was aware of Azrel's presence above them, and somehow, she thought the Angelus was listening.

"That is why I despise you," Sartish whispered. He stood and climbed up to check one of the topsails. Bella's eyes followed him, her insides twisted with a strange emotion.

In the days that followed, Bella noticed a change in him, as if this encounter had exorcised something. As taciturn and distant as ever, his hostility faded to something like indifference. Jonah must have noticed, because after lunch one day, he brought out a chart on a golden cylinder with ornate ends. As he spread the parchment on the deck, Bella drew in her breath.

It was a map of Mysterion, rendered in elegant black ink.

"That's where you both came from," Jonah said, pointing to the western side of the map and an island where Bella recognized a sketch of Leviathan. "And here is where we are going." Jonah moved his finger across the map, past the drawing of the Blind Watchman alone on his island, the mermaids, and the Elder's Island. "To the Edge of Mysterion and the Okean Falls."

Sartish leaned forward. Sensing his interest, the dropping of his guard, Bella allowed herself to talk.

"I thought Okean was up there." She pointed at the sky.

Azrel answered from the masthead. "It circles Mysterion, like a stream. It rises from the western desert, then up and over and down into the east. From there it goes downward to where the Lethes are buried, and up again into Mysterion. A complete circle, though not really."

"What do you mean, not really?"

"It's not really a circle as humans think of it. That's just the way we have to talk about it because you can't understand anything in more than three dimensions." The Angelus shook her head.

"So how does someone go back down... there?" Bella asked, feeling the tension return in her again.

Jonah glanced at Sartish. "If you leap off the Edge, Okean will carry you back to your sleeping place. No matter how long you have been in Mysterion, when you return to your sleeping, no time at all will have passed. You just continue doing what you were doing at the moment you left."

Bella felt a tide of curiosity carrying her on. "And what happens then?"

"It depends," Jonah replied.

"On what?"

"On what you choose to do next. You can learn how to kindle the Lamp and return to Mysterion, fully awake, or else..." he paused, "you can simply allow the memory of Mysterion to fade, like a dream."

"Kindle the Lamp," Bella said. "You mean, the lamp you held?"

"By that Lamp, yes."

"And how am I supposed to get that Lamp?"

"You don't need to. I'll find you. Or rather, the *Lamp* will find you."

Bella remembered the Seeing Pool where she had seen herself and Jonah talking in the cemetery. She felt her anger and frustration at him bubble to the surface again.

"So that's why you wanted me to come with you?" she said. "That was the second chance? Believe everything you say, jump off the Edge of Mysterion, and if I survive, forget everything I am here as some kind of illusion—all on the off chance that I could learn about your stupid lamp and come back as one of your slaves?" She laughed. "How stupid do you think I am?"

"I don't think you're stupid," Jonah said, beginning to roll up the map. "This has been done before, believe it or not. Just ask Sartish." He gestured at Sartish, who until now had stared at the map with a dark fascination on his fierce features.

Sartish looked up and nodded. "That was in the time of the Elder," he mumbled, "when I left Hodoul. When I was one of the Lethes, my uncle burned me with cigarettes." Bella glanced at the marks on his forearms. *So that's what they are.* Sartish saw the look and folded his arms. "He was keeping me confined in my room when I was not working. That is where the Djinn was coming to me. He gave me an escape, and I took it." Sartish hesitated. "When they put me in the Tree, I dreamed my uncle was burning me until I was black and charred, over and over." He paused. "I found out later that *he*, Hodoul, came for me before the Tree had drained all my memories, because he thought I would be more useful to him that way."

"We think he came for you too, Isabella," Jonah said. "Did he?"

Bella remembered how Hodoul had come to visit when she came out of the Tree. And then there was what Dis said—*With this or without this, you are a great treasure to him.*

"Yes," she said. "He did."

"What other explanation is there?" Jonah said, as if he had overheard her mind. "Go on, Sartish."

Sartish sighed and continued. He told how he had become Hodoul's ward, tending to him all day and night because the king suffered permanent insomnia, until Sartish learned to sleep with his eyes open. He told how he had accompanied the king to parlay with the Princes and forged secret compromises that allowed mutual raids only when it was convenient, constructing fictitious conflicts whose only purpose was to distract the crews from their boredom.

He told of the nights in the secret basement of the king's house, when Hodoul needed to make an example of one of the men, not to kill, but to create a lasting impression of what he was willing to do. Bella shivered at this confirmation of the screams that had floated across the parlay square.

"One night," Sartish was saying, "he decided to use a branding iron to teach someone a lesson. I remembered Uncle Sat then, how he had burned me all the time. And that was enough. I was done. I made my escape, and sailed east. For a while, I thought was done for when the Blind Watchman got me, but someone helped me escape…" He glanced at Jonah, who smiled.

"I think we helped each other that day," Jonah said.

"And then the mermaids found me, just as they found you," Sartish said to Isabella. "And they brought me to Elder's Island. But that wasn't the end of my journey. I had to travel to the Edge of Mysterion, and I had to return to Uncle Sat and his cigarettes, until Jonah came with his Lamp…"

"And since then," Jonah said, "he's been one of the faithful ones, despite the occasional temptations of his past."

Bella, who had been listening with a growing feeling of being trapped in Sartish's story, now laughed. "Oh, really? Then why does he *still* want to kill you for Hodoul's reward, eh?"

Sartish's scowled. Jonah laughed and gripped his shoulder.

"There is a great difference between wanting and *willing*, Isabella," he said. "Sartish and I have spoken many times about his struggles. He understands the difference, but you have yet to discover it."

Chapter Seventeen

Bella woke to the sound of Azrel shouting on deck, "They're on us! They're on us!" Jonah called something in reply. Against the hull the water had taken on a different sound—urgent, almost frantic. Bella could tell from the angle of the hull that they were under full sail. *La Desirée* hummed like the low string on a violin as the wind pushed her on.

She slipped out of bed and pulled on her clothes. Pushing her tangled hair behind her ears, she ran out of the cabin and up on deck. Jonah was already at the helm. He greeted her with a grin.

"They made it at last," he said, gesturing aft with his chin.

In plain view, no more than fifty leagues aft, *La Justice* bore down upon them, every sail on her yards bulging.

Sartish's voice, strained and angry, descended from above. "I still don't understand how they surprised us!" He was working in the rigging of the mainsail, swinging around from line to line.

"They didn't," Azrel replied from her perch at the masthead. "I knew they would reach us today."

"Then why didn't you say something?" Sartish shouted.

Azrel shrugged in Jonah's direction.

"Because they need to know where we're going," Jonah said.

"You wanted him to find us." Sartish stated the fact.

"Of course," Jonah replied. "How else would Bella be able to get back to her friends?"

"So what now?" Sartish asked, glancing at Bella. "We just die? For her?"

Jonah rocked his head. "Not quite yet. You seem to have forgotten that we've reached the Edge."

Bella swung around. High above, stream-like currents streaked the surface of the sky, flowing downward. Lower, the air shivered and then ran down like wet paint, smearing and swirling to the line where the horizon should be. Where it collided with the ocean, a white wall rose up, a cloud of mist rolling and boiling, breaking the sunlight into multiple rainbows.

A faint, continuous roar drifted toward them in the wind—immense, but distant.

Sartish was staring at the Edge. To Isabella, he looked as if he was reliving something. "It is too late," he said at last. "They will catch us before we are even reaching the line of mist!"

Jonah smiled. "Only if they can follow us through the shallows."

Several leagues distant, the green of the ocean broke out into blue patches. In places, white foam marked the teeth of a reef beneath the surface.

Sartish turned to Jonah with narrowed eyes. "You know the way through?"

"With my eyes closed," Jonah said. Then, for no reason, he laughed.

Sartish looked back at the approaching pirate ship. It was close enough now that the name was visible on the bow. The crew crowded the railing, some of them waving swords and fire-rifles.

"Will we be reaching the shallows, though?" Sartish wondered.

"We won't if we keep talking," Jonah replied. "There's a topsail luffing, and we need every knot."

Sartish looked up to where the fore gaff fluttered above, spilling wind. All argument vanished. He snapped to life and shinnied upwards. A moment later, the fore gaff filled again. Sartish moved among the rigging, adjusting the lines before slipping down to the deck. "We need the spinnaker up, Your Highness," he said, glancing at Bella. "A reach won't do the trick."

"Good thinking," Jonah nodded, and spun the wheel counterclockwise. *La Desirée* turned off her broad reach. Her aft came up as the wind roared full at her stern. Behind them, *La Justice* matched her move. Bella wondered if Ah-Time was at the helm, or perhaps Disagree... Horror filled her. She was running from Disagree. And yet she was running from Hodoul also. Perhaps there was still a chance to show *him*, and all this could end.

At the bow, Sartish had opened a small hatch and was dragging the bulk of the spinnaker out onto the deck. Wrestling and slipping for several seconds in the mass of silk, he finally managed to get the hook on the lines. Then he was hauling up the sail, which fluttered and twisted in the force of the wind. Around him the sheets tangled, impeding his progress.

"Want to help?" Jonah asked Bella with a smile.

"Why should I?"

"No reason," Jonah shrugged. "Just wondered if you wanted to see Hodoul before I'm dead."

Bella looked at him, then back at *La Justice*, now almost within a fire-rifle's shot of Jonah. If the spinnaker didn't get up soon, it would be minutes before they were boarded.

And then she would stand before *him* again.

Just a little more time, she thought. She turned and strode aft to where Sartish still struggled with the sail.

He glanced up at her. "I'm fine," he said, and went back to wrestling with the slippery material.

"I'm sure you are," Bella replied. "And you'll be even finer hanging from the main yard of *La Justice*."

"You better go away," he hissed. "Now."

"You don't want my help?" Bella asked. "Fine, then." She turned away.

"Sartish!" Jonah's voice came from the helm.

Sartish looked back. On *La Justice*, the crew lined the railing. Snipers waited in the yards for firing range.

Sartish shifted his eyes from the oncoming ship to Jonah, then to

Bella.

"Find the foot of the spinnaker," he muttered. "I will keep working on the head."

Bella went to work. Together, they unwound the tangle of silk and rope. With Sartish guiding the head, the massive, balloon-like sail rose, spread, and bulged over the water. *La Desirée* leapt forward. Waves crashed down on them in regular, drenching succession.

Having closed the gap even further in the minutes they had lost raising the spinnaker, *La Justice* now seemed to be holding its distance. But even as Bella watched, the frigate adjusted its course to fall directly aft of *La Desirée*. Above, the spinnaker sagged, collapsed, then refilled before collapsing again. The other sails were doing the same now—catching the wind, then collapsing. Bella glanced at Sartish, and then back at Jonah. From their aghast expressions, she knew both of them had realized that *La Justice* had stolen their wind.

"Shallows ahead!" Azrel shouted from the masthead.

Sartish spun around. The patches of dark and light blue and the reefs were less than a league distant. Beyond them, the wall of mist and the thunder of Okean's stream falling toward the Edge.

"It's too late!" Sartish shouted back at Jonah. "They will be upon us before we are getting there!"

Jonah said nothing. He closed his eyes and continued to steer them toward the shallows as quickly as the fickle sails would allow.

Yards behind them now, *La Justice* was preparing to board. At the railing, men crowded with coils of rope and grappling hooks. And there, standing among them at the bows, familiar and incongruous as a mountain, was Disagree, staring across the water at them with a look that paralyzed Bella even as it knocked her heart loose.

"Trim! Trim!" Sartish shouted at her as the spinnaker fluttered and collapsed. Bella did not even turn around. Sartish exclaimed in exasperation and grabbed the line from her, pulling it in until the sail filled again. *La Justice* was angling off now to overtake them. But even as she did, the wind, no longer obstructed by her bulk, now fell with full force on *La Desirée*, and the sloop darted forward. All her sails snapped tight. White water exploded on her bow.

For an instant, *La Justice*'s bow was level with their stern. Then she began to fall back. Several men raised their fire-rifles, and for the first time, Bella wondered that they had not done so before now. Then, over the wind, she heard a faint shout. She tore her eyes from Disagree and looked aft. King Hodoul stood by Ah-Time, the helmsman. The king's bush of white hair tossed around, and his crumbling features stood out even from a distance. He leaned forward as if driving the ship onwards by the force of his will and slashed the air with his hand. He shouted again—a stentorian order.

He doesn't want them to fire, Bella thought. It didn't make sense, unless...

Hodoul was calling something forward again. Disagree turned his head, listening for a second before hefting the grappling hook above his head. The men around him retreated as the hook swung in a wide circle. Disagree released, and the hook arced high overhead, hit *La Desirée*'s aft deck with a crack, and caught in the railing. Bella felt a check in the sloop's movement.

"Sartish!" Jonah shouted. "I can't let go of the helm!"

Sartish was already running aft, and Bella saw he had a hatchet in his hand. Seeing him go, desperation rolled over her in a wave. Dis had thrown that line to her, and now Sartish was going to cut it.

Dis, she thought.

The paralysis that had overcome her dropped away, and she began to run after Sartish. Leaping over cleats and ropes with an agility she had almost forgotten after long weeks on board ship, she reached him just as he raised the hatchet over his head, about to bring it down.

"Bella!" Jonah called. Bella ignored him, grappling Sartish around the neck and pulling him backwards onto the deck. They wrestled for precious seconds as *La Desirée* bucked against her leash and *La Justice* began to close in. The crew stood on the railing, ready to leap.

"Reef on the starboard bow!" Azrel shouted above. At the helm, Jonah closed his eyes, and took a deep breath. He held it for a long moment, frowning slightly, as if trying to see something inside his head. Then, suddenly, he opened his eyes and spun the wheel. *La Desirée* turned, and a booming to starboard announced that they had just avoided the reef.

Sartish pinned Bella down at last. With his forearm on her throat, he groped around for the hatchet, found it, then leaped up and dove at the rail, slashing downward.

The rope parted with a crack. *La Justice* fell back and groaned as it mounted the submerged reef. Men tumbled off the railing and fell screaming into the foaming green water. At the helm, Ah-Time spun the wheel. The sails collapsed. Rigging twisted and snapped.

Only Disagree in the bow and Hodoul in the stern remained untouched by the chaos that descended on the ship, now dead in the water. Bella could feel both their eyes across the widening gap—Hodoul like a hand gripping at her, trying to hold her. Disagree's hand was a different sort—held out in a gesture that broke her at last.

She was curled up in fetal position and sobbing as Sartish stood over her, his face stony.

"Now do you see?" he asked Jonah.

"No," Jonah said. His eyes were still closed as he navigated the shoals and hidden reefs. The wall of mist loomed higher. Behind, the pirate ship was now anchored and riding easy.

"You saw what she tried to do," Sartish said.

Jonah opened his eyes and regarded Sartish. "Would you have done differently, Sartish Kutty?"

Sartish's mouth worked, trying to form an answer and finding none.

"You cannot dispense with your past so easily as that," Jonah said.

Sartish's face turned grey. He stared at Jonah's serene face, then down at Bella, who was still weeping. He choked out a groan and stumbled away to disappear below decks.

"If you would be so good as to lower the sails, Isabella," Jonah said. "We have almost arrived."

Bella sobbed.

"Don't worry," he murmured. "You will have one more opportunity to do what you came to do. However, if we do not get those sails down, we will all be going over the Edge, like it or not."

Still weeping, Bella raised her head. The mist bank was closer than she had expected, as if they were moving faster than their sails could drive them. She heard a rushing sound around them, an urgency in the current. She scrambled to her feet and looked over the rail. The water around the submerged barriers had turned to rapids, carrying them forward in a rush toward the Edge.

Bella went into action. Several minutes later, only the topsails remained. "Keep those up," Jonah said, as she made to lower them. "We will need some maneuverability."

Barely ten yards ahead, the mist bank swirled in and out on itself, as if something were boiling deep within it. As Bella fought to catch her breath from the furor of lowering the sails, the ship swept into the bank. The reefs and shoals and the anchored pirate ship vanished behind a curtain of mist. The current ran in a solid grey-green rush. The thunder of falling Okean blocked all incidental sounds.

"Get ready to weigh anchor!" Jonah shouted, pointing to the bow.

Bella ran forward and grasped a lever attached to the windlass.

"Now!" Jonah said. "Weigh anchor!"

Bella pulled the lever. With a clatter, the anchor dropped. For a moment, it seemed it might never reach the bottom, but with no more than a couple of coils left in the chain, it caught and came tight. *La Desirée* came up short against her new mooring and swung around. The topsails fluttered as the schooner turned up into the wind, tracing a wide pendulum path in the current. Then she came to rest, her bow pointed against the current that drove on past toward the Edge of Mysterion.

Chapter Eighteen

Bella moved down the passageway leading aft to the master's quarters. Around her the sloop creaked and rocked against the current. The water hurried past the hull in a steady gurgle and hiss, so Bella did not attempt to conceal the sounds she might make as she went. The switchblade hidden in her fist was cold and heavy and somehow alien. She gripped it harder. At Sartish's cabin, she paused and bent her head. He might be waiting behind the door for the telltale sound of her step. She allowed a full minute to pass before moving on. Reaching the master's cabin door, she eased the latch open and slipped in, clicking the door shut behind her.

The master's bed lay before her. A faint light descending from the portholes along the upper walls illumined the rest of the cabin—a small bureau of drawers built into the wall, narrow benches on either side of the bed, and a tiny door she supposed led to a miniscule bathroom.

Jonah lay on his back, covered only with a sheet. From the way his hands were folded on his chest and the expression of humorous indifference on his lips, Bella imagined he was already dead. Then a faint snore emerged from his lips.

Her hands drenched in cold sweat, even in the stifling heat, she opened the switchblade and stepped up to the bed.

He opened his eyes and regarded her. "I had that dream about you again."

"I don't care," Bella said.

"You never asked what I dreamed. Why is that?"

"Are you deaf? I'm not interested in your stupid dream."

"Then grant me a dead man's wish," he said with a playful smile, "and let me tell you what it was."

"If you think more talk is going to change my mind..." Bella pressed the point of the blade against Jonah's bare chest. He winced slightly at the prick but made no move to avoid the contact. A solid black spot emerged in the gloom where the tip broke his dusky skin.

"No," he said with a tinge of breathlessness. "I just thought you might want to know why I allowed this."

Bella held the point in place, gathering herself to drive the blade into his heart.

"Why would I care?" she said.

"Because my willingness was an obstacle to you. Probably the most implacable enemy you have faced. Only the sight of your friend this afternoon, the desire to return to him, overcame it at last."

Bella stared at him. "How do you..." She shook her head. "Never mind! You have one minute to explain."

"I dreamed you were running in the darkness," Jonah said. "There were trees around, branches whipping at you, but I couldn't see them. I was looking down on you, as if I were flying above. And that man, the big one who stood behind Hodoul, your friend..."

Bella shivered, pressing the point harder, turning the black spot on Jonah's chest into a little rivulet that trickled down his side and onto the mattress. Jonah winced and went on. "He was running beside you, but you could not see him because he was away to one side, parallel and hidden by the trees. There was a light ahead, a house. Your friend angled away, and I could see him going on up the hill toward a hidden place where he could rest. But you ran on to the house and climbed through one of the windows.

"In the next moment—you know how dreams are—I was looking down inside the room, and you were curled on a bare mattress like an unborn infant. I could hear people shouting nearby, a man and a woman—your parents—and you were holding your head and trying to shut out their noise. But you couldn't do it, and you began to rock from side to side more and more. Then you looked up and screamed that it was my fault, it was all my fault." He stopped speaking and smiled at her. "And that was the dream. That was how I knew you would be coming to kill me, and that was how I recognized your friend."

Bella was pale, her knife arm extended, as if it had been frozen there.

"I know who you want to be, Isabella Morgan." Jonah spoke very softly. "And I know who you *are*."

Tears spilled out of her eyes. Her mouth opened, but several more seconds passed before words emerged. "I can't."

"Then don't."

"No," Bella said. She flung the switchblade onto the carpet. She went to the door and looked back, her face twisted. "I don't deserve to live. I failed and I'm going back to face it, that's all!"

Jonah said nothing. She turned her back on him. Throwing open the door, she raced down the passageway, not caring if Sartish heard her, and then up the steps onto the deck. A wind of mist-fine rain swept over her, cool after the oppressive heat below. She looked up to the masthead. Azrel had not returned. Bella felt a trace of relief that she would not have to endure the Angelus's sarcasm. However, even the thought of it brought the hot and bitter bile of shame in her throat, and she hurried aft.

Hand over hand, she hauled the skiff in. It came, and she wondered if she could pull hard enough to make any progress against the current. But it was too late to hesitate now.

She climbed into the skiff, set the oars, and released the line. The current pulled her aft the sloop. She pulled hard, and her regress slowed. Stationary for a moment, she regained the distance she had lost by increments until the skiff came level with *La Desirée* again. Bella dipped and hauled, her body aching and drenched with sweat and mist. After long minutes of effort, the sloop fell aft. The mist curtains drifted across, concealing the ship from view.

At last, Bella became aware that the current was easing as she put more distance between the skiff and the Edge of Mysterion. The skiff's movements took on a less strained quality, the bow making more and more progress through the short waves. The mist bank, too, receded, and white stars pricked out above her. The moon broke out above, spreading a sheet of light on the ocean. Mere feet behind her, the wall of mist rose up, lit up and swirling against the moonlight.

She was clear. Fighting to catch her breath and calm the wild beating of her heart, Bella rested on the oars and looked around. Almost at once, she spotted *La Justice* drifting a hundred yards ahead. There was something both ghostly and predatory about her, like a memory of a hundred raids coalesced into a single ship. Bella shivered. She knew they would spot her before she reached them, but she was surprised at how close she came before a low voice called out, "Identify yourself!"

"It's Couteau," she replied as steadily as she could manage. "Bella Couteau. I request parlay!"

There was a brief silence. A rope ladder dropped over the side, unrolling as it went. Bella grabbed a rung and clambered upwards. On the deck, shadowy figures immediately surrounded her.

"I want parlay," she repeated.

From directly ahead of her, a deep familiar voice rumbled, "I never believe I hear that from you, little Bella."

Bella began to tremble. "Dis?"

Disagree moved forward, a mountain of a shadow. "That's my name."

Bella ran forward and threw herself into her friend's arms. Her sobs came in great heaves and gulps, as if she had surfaced from a great depth. Disagree held her as if he had been carved there for all time.

Someone said, "Your little friend come home, eh?" A round of snickers echoed around them. Bella detached herself.

"He's expecting me, isn't he?" she asked Disagree.

"Of course," Disagree replied. "He knows you come." She could not tell his expression in the darkness.

"Then take me to him."

As Disagree led the way, the crew parted. They descended the steps.

The passageway was unlit except for a thin strip under the master's cabin door, which only exacerbated the darkness until it crushed Bella's heart. The snakes had come alive in her stomach again.

Disagree knocked at the Master's cabin door. At the muffled assent, he pushed it open, standing aside. His face was as impassive as ever, but she noticed the strained lines of exhaustion around his eyes. Reaching out to touch Dis's arm as she passed, Bella stepped through the doorway.

King Hodoul sat in the center of the cabin, wearing a simple linen nightshirt. His disordered curls glinted in the light of oil lamps. Before him a table was laid with platters of fruit, steaming crabs in their shells, and a roasted red snapper garnished with breadfruit fritters. A loaf of bread lay at his elbow, along with a flagon of palm wine and two brimming goblets.

His face reminded her of an eroded gravestone as he picked up one of the cups and raised it to her in greeting.

"I waited to have dinner," he said. "Now that you are here, we can eat."

Chapter Nineteen

King Hodoul gestured Bella to a stool beside his carved chair and said, "Thank you, Disagree. I will call when we need you."

"I want him to stay," Bella said.

A corner of Hodoul's mouth twitched. "You and I have some important matters to discuss, young lady. Things may be said that may make it difficult for you to remain friends with Disagree."

"I don't care. I want him to stay."

"I go," Disagree muttered.

Bella's eyes pleaded with him. "Please, Dis."

Disagree hesitated, then glanced at the pirate king. Hodoul shrugged. "Stay then. Just keep your mouth shut."

"He can say whatever he wants," Bella said.

"He can keep his mouth shut!" Hodoul slammed his hand down on the table, his face white with rage. "Or he *will* leave, and you will get what you deserve! Do you understand me?"

Bella stared at him, her jaw clenched and her heart racing.

"Sit down," Hodoul told her. He ignored Disagree, who closed the door and stood immobile in the corner.

"Now," Hodoul said. "Tell me one thing. Is he dead?"

Bella said nothing, looking down in her lap.

Hodoul nodded. "I thought not..." He was silent, then said, "Have some crab."

Bella hesitated, and the king's mouth twitched again. He placed two steaming crabs on her plate and then served her fish and fritters. Then he gestured for her to eat before tucking into his own plate.

Bella took her first spoonful reluctantly, but she soon got lost in the rich and spicy flavors in which she could detect Disagree's hand. He had overseen the great feasts the king had thrown following successful raids. Great trestle tables piled like this, encircling a great bonfire around which drunken Brethren leapt and whirled in absolute abandon with their female partners, sometimes falling into the flames to be dragged out again, singed and smoking, shrieking with laughter and pain. She tasted something both sweet and bitter in those memories now, as if she had lost them forever.

Across the room, Disagree seemed to mirror her mixed enjoyment of the food. At one moment, he regarded her with what she thought was pleasure. Then the lamp flickered and he seemed sad, almost pitying. The light shifted again, and he was inscrutable as always.

Bella shook her head.

Hodoul too was looking at her now, smiling. "You can taste it again, eh? I told him you would. Didn't I, Dis?"

Disagree nodded slightly. "I do it—she remember."

"That crab was just perfect, too," Hodoul kissed his bunched fingers. "If you boil them too long in the coconut milk, they get soggy. But not this, not this..." Then he fell silent, admiring the food.

"Remarkable creatures, robber crabs," he murmured. "Not only delicious when cooked in milk and spices, but admirable characters as a whole. I saw one climb a tree once, pick a nut, climb down, and open it within a minute. Another time, I saw a fellow chasing one because it had stolen a piece of his wife's jewelry. He cornered the creature, used a club to try to get the jewelry, but you think that crab lost out? It turned and chased the fellow right back to his house with the bracelet or whatever it was held as tight as ever in its claw." Hodoul chuckled and rocked back in his chair, looking at Bella through lowered eyelids.

"Enterprising creatures," he continued. "*Strong* creatures, you know? But the really interesting thing is—" he raised one finger "—and I want you to listen carefully, my dear Bella, the interesting thing is that the robber crab does not start off strong. Do you know how they start off life, hmm?"

Disagree shifted in the corner, and Bella glanced at him before answering the king, "No, I don't know."

"They start as *hermit* crabs. You know those?"

An image flashed into Bella's mind—a hermit crab struggling on its back just before she brought her foot down on it. She had not realized how that insignificant act of cruelty had stuck with her.

"Despicable creatures," Hodoul was saying. "Scurrying from shell to shell, fighting over the skeletons of the dead." He shook his head. "A waste of the Wind's creative energy, if you ask me. And for its infancy, at least—" he emphasized these words "—the robber crab resembles one of these hermits. It too is small and uses a borrowed shell to protect itself from predators. But the key difference is that unlike hermit crabs, which aren't real crabs at all, by the way..."

Bella looked toward Disagree, thinking, *What is he going on about?*

"Forgive me." Hodoul's voice drew her eyes back. "I do love a good analogy. Almost done, if you will indulge me."

Bella shrugged. "I have time." She did not understand where this new confidence was coming from.

"Not quite as much as you think," Hodoul murmured. "But we will come to that. Now, what was I saying?"

"Hermit crabs are not real crabs," Bella muttered. She picked up a breadfruit fritter and took a nibble.

Hodoul nodded. "That's right. Hermit crabs never acquire a shell of their own. They're always scurrying from one borrowed home to another. And if they can't find a bigger shell, they don't grow any bigger. And then they can be eaten, much as I eat these crabs right now." He paused with a grin, and the meaning behind his words came to Bella like the shadow of a shark beneath the water. The nervous tension from before flooded back into her.

"But the robber crab is different. When it is old enough and strong enough, it emerges from its shell. And then it is free to do whatever it pleases, and no one can touch it." Then he broke off with a laugh and picked up a claw. "Well, almost no one, anyway. *Everyone* has a natural predator."

He cracked open the claw with his teeth before sucking out the flesh. He dropped the shell into a bowl now overflowing with broken remains, and wiped his mouth, his eyes never leaving Bella's face.

"Do you see my point?" he said.

"No," Bella replied, though she felt uneasy now.

Hodoul leaned forward. "Well, let me give you a hint. What is that you are wearing around your neck?"

Bella looked at him, caught off guard. "What do you mean?"

"Don't play with me!" Hodoul snapped. "Around your neck! What is it?"

Bella touched the place where her medallion hung. "It's mine."

"Show it to me."

Bella hesitated, staring at him.

"Show it to me!"

Bella pulled out the medallion on its cord. It hung against her shirt, glowing warmly in the lamplight.

"What is it?" Hodoul asked.

Bella hunched her shoulders. "A doubloon. It's mine, I didn't steal it!"

"I didn't say you did. But do you remember where you got it?"

Bella was chewing on her fingernail now. "My father gave it to me. Before..."

"Before you came to Mysterion."

"Yes."

"It was one of his few gifts to you, wasn't it?" He was leaning close now, eyes glittering in the broken face.

Bella felt a dizziness come over her as she stared at the pirate king. "How did you know that?" she whispered.

"I can tell you more than that. I can tell you that it belonged to one of your ancestors, a pirate. That it was passed from generation to generation. That it was a constant reminder to your family of their origins, a point of pride that they came from bold adventurers, plunderers, *robbers.*"

Hodoul's face filled Bella's vision, blocking out the rest of the room. Somewhere nearby she could feel Disagree, somehow locked out now behind the overwhelming presence of the pirate king. Somewhere inside her she could hear her father's voice, very far away—*Remember where you came from, my girl. It wasn't always we were like this, living in crap. We were strong.*

"Do you know the name of the pirate to whom that doubloon once belonged?" Hodoul asked, almost gently.

Bella shook her head, but she did. It all made sense now. Hodoul nodded, having seen the answer in her eyes.

"Only one other person knows the story of how I came to Mysterion," he said, glancing at Disagree. "It happened on the day I was hanged for piracy. They brought me out to the main square. There was a good crowd that day, the best they ever had, I was told." A bitterness tinged his smile. "They read the verdict—piracy, rapine, murder, and so on and so forth. Then they asked if I had anything to say. I asked them to free my hands. At first they wouldn't do it, but I convinced them in the end. So I stood there looking down at those landlubbers. Then I took that coin—" he pointed at the medallion "—and held it up in the air so they could all see it. Then I said, 'Find my treasure, whoever is able!' and I threw it into the crowd."

The silence that filled the cabin pressed down on Bella like a solid thing. She was paralyzed by it.

"I didn't just throw that coin at random, though," Hodoul continued. "I wasn't going to let just *anyone* have it. I threw it to my beloved Natalie, who had stood by me in all the years of my wanderings. She didn't hide herself away that day, either. She stood right at the front, and hers was the only face free from disgust in that crowd. She alone showed some pride at that moment, and I saw her catch that doubloon and hide it in her bodice before anyone knew what was happening. She was always good at making gold disappear." He chuckled.

"In the uproar, they led me to the gallows. That was where the Djinn came to me, disguised as the hangman. How could I resist? He held out the pendant, and I took it just before they opened the trapdoor."

Hodoul's words sank into silence. His face seemed to recede, and Bella could see Disagree in the corner again.

"You probably know that those who return to the lower world return to the moment they left," Hodoul said. He did not wait for her response. "If I ever go back, I will go back to the moment I died. Which is why I can do things here that living people would never dare to do. Do you understand?"

Bella tried to nod, but she still could not move.

"But of course, everyone wants continuation, progeny. Even people like myself. Which is why, when the Djinn summoned me and informed me that they had imprisoned someone wearing that medallion around her neck, I was more than interested. We made a little trade, they and I. They got something I had been willing to give up a long time ago."

"What was it?" Bella asked in spite of herself.

"What was it?" he echoed, staring at Bella. "That is not your concern! All you need to know is, in exchange, I got you with your memory intact, so you could be useful still, not just one of those—" he gestured at the deck above them "—those dregs. You could still remember a little of your life in the lower world, enough, anyway, to know how you got that medallion and perhaps even how important it was."

He paused a moment to let the words sink in. "And when the time was right, I could find a reasonable, a legal way to bequeath my achievement in Mysterion to you. The assassination of Jonah provided just such an opportunity. I thought the choice between exile and death—" he lifted his left hand "—or an act of daring and an inconceivable reward—" he raised his right hand "—would be just the thing to motivate you." Then he looked between them. "I thought your limited options would be sufficient to put a little steel in your back when you weakened, but..." He allowed the rest of the sentence to drift away, his eyes now baleful and cold.

"Which brings me to my little excursus about crabs," he continued. "You see, my dear Bella, I think I understand why you hesitated to do what you knew you had to do with Jonah. When you joined them, they convinced you that you're really one of them—a little hermit crab. And because you are young and impressionable, and perhaps you feel as if you are weak inside, you started to think the shell you had crawled into was really your own. But it wasn't, you see." Hodoul's voice rose to a shout. "Because you are *not* a hermit crab! You are a robber crab, and you have been *since the very beginning*! Am I making myself clear?"

Bella's head jerked. Hodoul's eyes now gripped her face.

"You cannot escape the past, my little robber crab. And that is why you will go back now and complete your task. You *will* do it and you *will* receive the gift I am offering you! Or else I may have to conclude that you are not who I thought you were, that you really are a hermit crab. And in that case, I will have no trouble in eating you alive and consigning myself to damnation."

Hodoul sat back and drank from his goblet. His breaths came hard, his face flushed.

"I have nothing more to say to you," he said at last. He told Disagree, "Take her back to her boat and let her go."

Disagree spoke for the first time, and Bella heard the strain in his voice. "Your Majesty, I say something."

"I don't want to hear it. Just do as you are told!"

Disagree met Hodoul's implacable stare for an instant before lowering his head and leading Bella into the dim hallway. They climbed back on deck, where the crewmen huddled in groups. They crowded forward, firing questions at Disagree from every direction.

"What did he say?"

"She'll be hanged, no doubt?"

"Or keel-hauled, right?"

Disagree silenced them with a sweeping gesture.

"The girl has business for His Highness, and none is yours."

"Come on, Disagree. Give us a word!"

But Disagree turned to stone again, pushing forward so that they had no choice but to give way before him while they muttered about favoritism, and who the hell gave him the right to keep things from them, and if it weren't for the Code, they would tickle him into talking with a dagger. When they reached the ladder, Disagree turned to Bella for the first time. She was aware of the men crowding from every side. Their stink was overwhelming.

"When you finish your job," he said, "you light a beacon at the masthead. I come to get you then."

"Bring a skiff," Bella muttered, shivering. "The current's too strong."

"You letting her go?" someone cried.

"He's letting a traitor go!"

Disagree's head found the source of the voice. "Shut up, Cauchemar."

"Or what?" Cauchemar replied.

"Come here and you see," Disagree replied.

Cauchemar pushed his way forward, a square-shaped man with a scar that left his mouth in a permanent grin.

He leered up at Disagree. "What now, Monsieur Disagree?"

Without warning and without any effort at all, Disagree grabbed Cauchemar by the throat and lifted him into the air. He swung him over the side and let go. With barely enough time to scream and clutch at Dis's hand, Cauchemar hit the water with a loud explosion. He sank at once and a second later resurfaced, screaming and flailing and slapping at the surface.

"He can't swim!" someone shouted.

"Then you best get him," Disagree said, "and let me follow my orders."

He turned away as the crewmen scrambled to man ropes and rescue the hapless Cauchemar.

"Go now," he said to Bella.

"Come with me," she said. Her voice was quivering.

"No," Disagree said. "I need to stay with him."

"Why?" Bella cried.

"Because everyone needs someone," Dis said. "Even him. He thinks I am his slave, and so I must be a slave, for him. But you," he added, regarding her. "You think you are not his slave, but you are."

Bella knew it was true. She was precious to Hodoul, all right—just as all possessions are precious.

All this was a lie, she thought. The flame that had been guttering inside her went out. Disagree reached out and lifted her over the rail. Her feet found the rungs of the ladder, and she reached out to steady herself with one hand, while clinging to Disagree's arm for a moment with the other.

"Please, Dis," she begged. "Please come."

With a strength far beyond hers, Disagree pulled her hand off his arm and planted it on the ladder.

"I have my path," he said. "You have yours."

The men had succeeded in hoisting Cauchemar over the side, and now he lay coughing and heaving on the deck.

"You almost killed the bugger, Disagree," someone commented. "Not that he didn't deserve it, mind you."

"When we get back," Cauchemar rasped between coughs, "you can start digging your own grave, black man."

"Go now," Disagree growled at Bella. "They start up again." He turned to Cauchemar's sodden form. "So, you want some more lessons. Let's go then." Cauchemar wailed and the men drew back. Feeling as if her flesh were tearing with each movement, Bella climbed down the ladder and leapt into the skiff. Fumbling with the ropes, she untied the bow-line, and the boat drifted away from *La Justice*. She manned the oars and began to pull, though she had no idea where she was going or how she was going to find *La Desirée* again. Still, her arms kept pulling, and though it felt as if she were rowing through tar, *La Justice* soon fell behind. The first fingers of mist drifted past. A white hand closed around the boat, blotting out the panorama to aft. The moon vanished, the stars overhead were blotted out.

Bella became aware of something behind her. She looked over her shoulder. Azrel's familiar light floated in the mist. It was dim, barely more than a brighter patch of mist, but unmistakable.

Confusion assailed her. Had they known she was coming? But why would they guide her back, unless... She could not find the reasons, but somehow she knew this was her last hope of refuge.

The current carried the skiff forward. Bella used the oars to keep the skiff pointed at Azrel's beacon. As she approached, Azrel's light dimmed. The Angelus was taking no chances, keeping her light as faint as possible on the off-chance the pirates caught a glimpse of their location.

La Desirée loomed out of the darkness. Bella angled off, pulled in the oars, and reached out just in time to grab the rope ladder hanging amidships. She shinnied up the ladder. Once over the railing, she secured the line on a cleat and paused a moment to catch her breath.

She looked up at Azrel. "Thank you."

"Not my choice," the Angelus replied, and dimmed herself almost to extinction.

He told her to guide me back, Bella thought. She felt her heartbeats speed up. Something thrashed inside her.

A dark shape, more solid than Jonah's, appeared from below decks.

"Coming to finish it off?" Sartish's voice shook with emotion.

Bella was suddenly shaking. "I want to see Jonah."

"You will have to be killing me first!" Sartish replied.

Until that moment, Bella had not known what she was going to do.

"You don't understand," she said, stepping into an abyss. "I want to stay."

Chapter Twenty

Bella stood at the railing, looking down at Jonah and Sartish in the skiff. Azrel fluttered around, agitated.

"Is this wise, Your Highness?" the Angelus said for the third time.

"There's no other way, Azrel," Jonah replied. He smiled up at Bella. "This is why we are here."

"I know," Azrel said, "but—"

"I am still not believing it," Sartish declared. "What's the game?" he asked Bella. "What did he hatch this time, eh?"

Bella was shaking and no words would come out. She just shook her head.

"That's enough, Sartish!" Jonah snapped.

Sartish hunched his shoulders, glanced at Jonah, and muttered something. Jonah ignored him, looking up at Bella with an expression she did not recognize.

"What will you do?" he asked, though she had explained everything beforehand.

Bella shrugged, feeling tears welling up within her again.

"Are you sure?"

"Even a real hell is better than a beautiful lie," Bella said.

Jonah took a deep breath and nodded.

"I will see you," he said.

Bella folded her arms. "Whatever you say. Now go before I change my mind!"

Jonah raised his hand, but Sartish did not look at her. The skiff pulled away and disappeared into the mist.

Bella said nothing, nor did she raise her hand in response. She felt as if every living being had deserted the universe and every source of light had been put out. Several minutes passed before she became aware of a presence above. Azrel sat at the masthead, looking down at her, serene as a statue.

"What do you want?" Bella asked.

"I'm staying here," Azrel replied.

"I don't understand."

Azrel looked at her for a long moment before responding. "Do you know what an Angelus is?"

Bella shook her head.

"We are witnesses," Azrel said. "From the beginning of the People, we have watched and listened and borne witness to your life. At times, we conversed with humanity and even got involved, but that is not our first task. Our first task is to see everything, to witness to everything. We gather events, moments of sadness and horror, laughter, silliness..." The Angelus's voice drifted away.

"I have seen infants born and infants die, old people die and old people born also." She laughed. "I get sarcastic because that's who I am. Every Angelus has a way of letting off steam. Some say nothing, some weep, others get angry or laugh. Me, I can't help but see the irony in everything. I have to roll my eyes because if I didn't, I couldn't stand it anymore. I'd have to run away above the heavens."

"So that's why you're here," Bella interjected. "To *spy* on me?"

Azrel chuckled. "We always see," she said, "so what you do may be known."

"Who cares about what I do anyway?"

"Everything matters," Azrel replied. "Everything must be gathered in so that the story may be told in the Higher Mysterion. That is what we have been given to do—we gather so the Wind can tell."

"Whatever you say," Bella said. "Just don't watch me, that's all!"

Azrel tilted her head. "What are you afraid of?"

"I am not afraid. I'm..."

Azrel tilted her head. "What?"

She had to force the word out. "Ashamed."

"Ashamed of what?"

"Betrayal. Failure. I was weak..." Tears flowed down her cheeks.

"Weakness is not such a bad thing," Azrel said.

"Yes," Bella shouted back. "Yes, it is!"

"So why did you come back?"

Bella just shook her head. Azrel sighed and looked off into the distance. The thunder from the Edge of Mysterion filled the silence. Azrel looked down again.

"So you want me to leave you," the Angelus said.

Bella nodded, thinking, *No, please stay...*

Azrel inclined her head. "Then I will go. But I will still watch from above."

"Why can't you just go away?"

"I told you," Azrel said, "everything must be seen. You have always been seen, from the beginning. For example—" a mischievous smile crossed her lips "—you were seen—not by me, someone else—when you stole Dragon's claw powder from Joe Granbousse and then smoked it."

Bella felt her face growing hot.

"You want to be alone," Azrel continued. "You always have. But no one is alone, Isabella. At least not now."

"If you have to watch, then watch," Bella said. "Just don't let me see you. I can't stand your face anymore!"

Azrel shook her head and clicked her tongue. "That would really hurt, if my face were not just something I put on to give you humans something to look at. Oh well, I know when I'm not wanted." She floated upward without perceivable effort. "Goodbye Isabella," she called down. "And may you find some use for your weakness after all. Such a waste, otherwise. Either way, I will keep watch." She faded into the streams of mist and darkness.

Bella sat down and hugged her knees as a hurricane of emotion descended on her. She gripped tighter, as if trying to crush herself, and when this did not succeed, she stood up and paced the deck. At last, she stopped in front of the mast and looked up. She knew there was a lamp up there. It had remained unlit at night while they had Azrel, but now it awaited a single lit match.

"Light a beacon," Dis had said. "I come for you."

Bella fumbled around in her pockets but found them empty. She ran below, fumbling in pitch-dark cabins until she located a box of matches in a galley cupboard. She found something else, too—a small hatchet—before climbing back up on deck. She ran to the bow and hid the hatchet within easy reach.

Amidships again, she clambered up the mast until she was swaying back and forth, while mist-laden gusts swept over her. After several attempts, she kindled the lamp, and a sphere of light pushed back the darkness. She knew it would not be long now before the king came for her.

And then... she thought. A fit of shivering overcame her, so violent she almost lost her balance. She was cold now, and not just from the mist. She climbed down to the deck and made her way to the bow. The chain that anchored *La Desirée* was taut as a bar, the only thing preventing her from being swept toward and over the Edge of Mysterion. Bella leaned back against it, staring out to the edge of the lamplight.

The splash of an oar came to her over the distant thunder and the sounds of the wind and current. It was close, but Bella found it difficult to tell how close. She stood still. Every nerve ending in her body seemed to have acquired the gift of sight and now stared into the mist.

A skiff broke out of the darkness, shadowy in the lamplight, driving down the current past *La Desirée*. Bella recognized the massive figure at the oars at once—Disagree. Joy flooded through her, only to be twisted into terror as she saw another figure in the aft, hunched and unmistakable.

Disagree worked the oars to bring the skiff around against the current, then pulled her back until she came amidships with *La Desirée*. With a crab-like movement, Hodoul slipped forward and grabbed the rope ladder. Leaving Disagree to secure the skiff, he hauled himself up and onto the deck. A moment later, Disagree pulled himself over the edge and took his customary place behind Hodoul, facing Bella. She waited for them in the bow.

"Where are they?" Hodoul said.

"They're gone," Bella replied, her voice trembling. "I let them go."

The pirate king chuckled—it was not a pleasant sound. "You dared to defy me," he said. Drawing his rapier, he stepped forward. Disagree reached out and grabbed his shoulder, preventing him. Hodoul whipped around. As his dagger swept backward, Bella grabbed the hatchet at her feet and raised it high over the taut anchor chain.

"Don't!" she shouted. Hodoul paused and turned. He turned back to her, sheathing the rapier.

He chuckled again, this time with genuine mirth. "You must be joking, Bella Couteau. You would dare to send us all over the Edge? You would go back to being one of those pathetic Lethes? I appreciate a heroic gesture as much as the next man, but this is just silly. Besides, you'd need to cut more than once to get through that chain, and by then we'd be on you. So why don't you put down your little piece of foolishness and let's try to talk as adults, all right?"

Bella did not move, but the hatchet swayed in the air. Hodoul saw the movement and nodded. "You see? I can be reasonable, too. Do you think I would kill my own flesh and blood? Really, now."

"You'd kill anyone who crossed you!"

Hodoul shook his head. "My only descendant? My posterity in this life? You must think I have no humanity left. No, I would never do that. A little punishment perhaps. What is life without consequences, after all? But death is out of the question. I swear it on Leviathan."

"You expect me to believe that I would come back and not be in your debt for the rest of my life?" Hodoul said nothing, staring at her, and Bella went on. "Since when were you giving away forgiveness? I know better than that. I know what your 'mercy' costs!"

"I don't know what you mean," Hodoul said.

"Tell him, Dis," Bella said. Her arm was starting to hurt, so she lowered the hatchet, resting it on the railing. Hodoul's eyes followed the movement all the way down, but he did not make a move.

"Tell him," Bella repeated. Disagree said nothing. "Fine, then I will." She addressed Hodoul, surprised at the sudden calm that descended on her. "Dis told me that when he came to the Brethren, long before me, he was alone. No one would call a small fat black boy 'Brother,' so they chased him and beat him, but you did nothing about it. Then one day, some other boys tried to hang him. They almost did it, but you happened on them and they ran away. You brought him down, and when he was better you told him you rescued him, but you never punished the ones who tried to kill him. Not even a lashing. You disobeyed your own law..."

"How dare you hold *my* law over my head!" Hodoul shouted.

"And you indebted him to you. He believed he owed you his life!"

"He did. I rescued him!"

"You think he's a fool?" Bella retorted. "He found out what really happened, but he stayed with you. You know why?"

"I think you had better stop talking," Hodoul hissed.

"Because he believes everyone needs someone who loves them. Even you!"

The pirate king's tone was mocking. "Oh, that's so touching, I think I might just have a good cry. Isn't it touching, Dis?" He looked at Disagree, who moved his head in a way that Hodoul took for assent. He swung back to Bella. "You see? You think Disagree is a child like you? He made his choice to stay loyal, and he has reaped the reward. Far more than if I had just left him hanging." He snickered at the joke. "So what if I showed a little mercy to those scamps? That is my right as king of the Brethren. I won't be lectured by some immature little turd who thinks she can stand up to me just because I told her we're related! Don't presume on me, Bella Couteau. My patience has almost run out. Drop that hatchet and come back with us. I can still prevent you from suffering the full consequences of your gross error, but only if you do exactly as I say—right now. This is your last chance—wisdom or folly!"

Bella looked at him, then raised the hatchet again. As it hung in the silence, Bella spoke. "Send Disagree to take it from me, or it comes down."

Hodoul did not hesitate. "Take it, Dis," he snapped. "Let's be done with this!"

Disagree took a step forward.

"Faster, man. Do it!"

Disagree continued on at his chosen pace, closing in on Bella. Three feet away from her, he stopped. Bella could feel his eyes pressing into hers—an almost unbearable weight.

"Take it!" Hodoul spoke each word.

"Yes," Bella said. "Take it, Dis. Take it all away from me."

Disagree took another two steps forward, reached out, and grabbed Bella's hand with his own, engulfing it. And that's where he stayed, holding up the hatchet with her, looking into her eyes.

"What are you doing?" Hodoul screamed.

Bella felt Disagree's hand, heavy around hers, pressing down. Her heart broke loose. She stared at him.

"You sentimental fool!" From the corner of her eye, Bella saw Hodoul start forward, drawing his sword.

"He's coming," she whispered to Disagree.

"Then cut it," he replied.

Her arm shivered, muscles aching under the almost dead weight of Dis's hand.

"I'm scared," she whimpered.

"Yes," he said. "That is alright."

"I'll teach you!" Hodoul shouted, striding forward, turning his blade flat to whip Disagree across the back.

"Now!" Disagree commanded, his voice louder than she had ever heard it. And at last, Bella gave in. She allowed her arm to collapse under the full weight of Disagree's arm, bringing the hatchet down. The blade sliced through the chain. It parted with a loud *crack!* and the sloop was free, slipping backward in the current toward the Edge of Mysterion.

Chapter Twenty-One

Hodoul froze, his arm in the very act of delivering the stroke to Disagree's back.

Disagree turned to him. "You get back in the skiff. Now."

La Desirée was swinging around in the current, the deck heeling as she drifted sideways, swifter now.

"You killed us," Hodoul whispered.

"Yes," Disagree agreed. "If you don't get into the skiff."

Even as his face crumbled with fear, the pirate king turned on Bella. "I should kill you where you stand!"

"Then you kill me too," Dis replied, "and you row that skiff yourself. *If* you can."

"You're going back with him?" Bella cried, grabbing his arm. "Dis..."

"Go," Dis told Hodoul, who stood panting with rage, his sword shaking. "I come behind you right now."

Bella shook Disagree's arm. "You're coming with me!"

"I won't let her back," Hodoul snarled. "Not even if she begs!"

"She do not want to," Dis said, ignoring Bella's pleading expression.

The roar of the Edge was louder now, though still out of sight. The mist too was thicker, more like an opaque wall of water. Any moment they would come to it. Nausea coated the back of her throat.

"Get in now," Disagree said to Hodoul.

The pirate king hesitated. "Are you coming?" he demanded.

Disagree nodded, and Bella felt herself grow cold.

"You'd better!" Hodoul snapped. "I can't believe you'd join her in this foolishness!" He turned on his heel and strode aft, holding onto the railing to balance against the wild movements of the ship. As he reached the ladder, he spun around. His face was pale in the tossing light of the masthead lamp.

He reached his hand out toward Bella. "Last chance, Couteau!" he shouted. "There's no mercy after this. You'll forget everything. You'll die an insignificant layabout on the street with two or three snotty brats hanging off you. I'm offering you one last chance. Against my better judgment, one more chance at greatness."

"Shut up!" Bella screamed. "Shut up!" She looked up at Disagree. "Please, Dis."

"No," Dis said. "You make this choice. You do not make it for me."

"But you're going back with him?"

Bella thought a smile crossed Disagree's face. "As you say," he said, "everyone need someone who love him."

She could find no reply for that.

"Disagree!" There was a definite note of fear in Hodoul's voice now.

"I come!" Disagree shouted. He placed his hand on Bella's shoulder. She threw her arms around him and clung until he disengaged her and lumbered back amidships to where Hodoul waited at the ladder. Seeing him come, the pirate king threw Bella one last poisonous look before disappearing over the railing. Disagree untied the bow-line, leaving a single loop to hold the skiff to *La Desirée*. Bella ran toward him. Hodoul had settled himself in the stern. Disagree pulled the boat close. The skiff rocked and tossed as he leapt on board.

"Careful, damn you!" Hodoul shouted in panic, perching on the transom. At last, she could see him for the pathetic figure he was, terrified and utterly dependent for his survival on Disagree, who ignored him as he set the oars to the oarlocks. When he was ready, he looked up at Bella, pale at the railing.

"When you come back I see you again," he said.

"Come back?" Hodoul cried. "She's not coming back!"

"You keep quiet!" Disagree roared. "Or we all go over!"

Hodoul was sullen, cowering in the stern.

Disagree looked up at Bella again. "You find me," he said.

Bella shook her head. "Dis."

"What?"

Then tears were streaming down her cheeks. "I love you."

Disagree nodded. "I love you also." He tossed the rope away from him. As it slipped up and around the railing, Bella caught and held onto it. The weight of the skiff dragged her forward.

"Let go," Disagree called.

Bella clung, then, with a shudder, dropped the line. Disagree wound it up, manned the oars, and hauled to work the skiff around against the current. For several seconds it seemed as if they made no progress. Disagree heaved with all his strength. The skiff fell behind.

La Desirée now drifted broadside to the current. The cacophony of the Edge beat on Bella's eardrums. The water streamed toward the precipice, dark and unblemished, with only the occasional flash of foam to indicate its speed.

The mist parted. Okean was a wall of water streaked with the light of the stars and the moon, stretching forever upward and to either side. At the level of the horizon, the foam was a solid barrier.

Looking aft, Bella saw the skiff at the edge of the mist-line and Hodoul gesticulating. Disagree pulled, exerting all of his immense strength. The skiff made incremental headway against the current and vanished back into the mist.

Feeling as if she had been separated from her body, Bella turned to face Okean. She ran aft and grabbed the spinning wheel. Straining, she worked *La Desirée* around until the sloop pointed at the Edge. No longer resisting the current, the ship slipped into Okean.

"I want to remember!" she shouted, but her voice was lost in the thunder. And then she was into the white explosion. Solid water thundered down over her, the ship breaking up before everything dropped away beneath her. Silence descended as she floated past the Edge into an endless waterfall of gold light, breathing an air far lighter than air.

Chapter Twenty-Two

Azrel descended through the mist bank to where Jonah and Sartish waited in the tossing skiff.

"She went over," the Angelus called.

Sartish shook his head in disbelief.

"She did," Azrel said. "I witnessed it."

"And you will remember?" Jonah said.

"I wouldn't give this away to anyone," Azrel replied. "This is mine."

"You see," Jonah told Sartish.

Sartish shrugged. "She won't be back."

"She will," Jonah said. "I will enter sleep now and go down to her among the Lethes. In time, she will come back. Azrel, take us to the nearest safe harbor. When I awake in the morning, we will have to find a way to deliver the island from the pirate siege."

"Yes, Your Highness." Azrel sighed.

As Jonah settled himself to sleep in the bottom of the skiff, the Angelus gestured at Sartish to toss her the bow-line. He hesitated. She clicked her tongue and descended to pick it up herself.

"I have to say," she declared, "it always amazes me that the Wind would choose such weaklings as the guides of Mysterion!" Radiant and fluttering, she took up the slack of the line on her shoulder. The skiff came around to follow the Angelus west, tossing its bow against the waves.

Curled up in the hull, his eyes half-closed, Jonah could just make out Sartish's face looking down at him with an expression he could not quite decipher. Jonah had just begun to wonder whether his friend was going to make it through, when sleep descended upon him.

Lethes III

Jonah inhaled with a gasp and opened his eyes.

He sat on the rocks above the beach, with the Angeli's Lamp on his knees. The sea glittered at him under the sun, and the monsoon breeze carried the cool tinge of salt water to his lips.

As it always did when he opened his eyes, the memory of Mysterion hovered in the back of his mind, like the after-image of something brilliant that had imprinted itself on his mind, then faded. Still, its presence was there, like a deep, quiet reservoir flowing beneath his consciousness.

Focusing on the present, he remembered Isabella and what his mother had recounted—Isabella's running away, her father being stabbed—but no trace of his former despair remained.

Today will be different, he thought. He could not explain why, but he was as certain of it as he was certain of breathing.

Several minutes later, Jonah turned off the sea road onto the road that climbed toward the mountain. Actually, it was not so much a road as a couple of parallel mud tracks, between which the grass grew almost knee-high. On either side, bushes and thorny vines threatened to overwhelm any sign of the tracks. Trees closed overhead, sealing in the heat of the morning.

The forest gave way to a clearing where the Morgans' house slumped, decaying on its stilts. Surrounding the building and in the spaces beneath the stilts lay the rusted parts of old cars, while further out in the yard entire wrecks sank into untended vegetation. Bred from stagnant pools, the mosquitoes were almost unbearable, hanging in visible clouds over the place and descending thickly onto Jonah's skin in spite of his best efforts to sweep them off.

A large dog, its fur falling off in patches, rushed out, barking and snarling. Having suffered a bite on his first visit, Jonah did not attempt to be friendly but kicked the animal as it leaped at him. The dog fell back yelping and ran off with its tail between its legs.

A short, skinny woman with a dried appearance and cropped dyed-crimson hair stood in the open doorway. The grey-blond roots showed clearly.

"So you came, eh?" she called in the voice of a heavy smoker. "Don't know why you bothered, my boy. She's not worth it, is what I say. But you might as well come in, now you're here."

He stepped inside. Charlene Morgan sat at the dining table, with the half-smoked cigarette pinched at the tips of her fingers. Clouds of smoke hung about her aged features. She gestured Jonah to the chair opposite.

"We're sick and tired of this, Jonah!" she said.

Jonah sat down at the table. Overflowing ashtrays and dirty plates cluttered the surface. From the far side of the room, Ray Morgan echoed his wife. "As the woman says, we're tired, my boy. Tired of trying with her." Slouched in a faded armchair, Isabella's father wore only a pair of shorts. The only clean spot on his skin was a bandaged patch on the left side of his chest. Under a tangle of blond hair that reminded Jonah of Isabella, Ray's dull grey eyes registered a permanent expression of surprise, as if he could not quite comprehend why life had dealt him this hand. Stimulated by the morning heat, rivulets of sweat already streaked his forehead.

"We give that girl everything," Ray declared. "Everything she wants, we give it to her if we can. Money, everything."

Everything but what she needs, Jonah thought.

"As a matter of fact," Charlene said, "that's what happened last night. She comes in with that face on—you know the one. She doesn't want to eat, just money she wants. More money from what I give her yesterday. I say no, because I know she give it to that layabout Maxim. I tell her if she wants cigarettes I have some. But no, just money. I say no again, and she starts screaming and throwing things like she always does. She gets so worked up by then that she goes to her room and she won't come out. What can I do?"

Charlene looked at Jonah as if he might know the answer. Seeing none in his face, she continued. "Then this one comes home," she jerked her head at Ray, "and he throws a nonsense. As if he could do any better!" She jabbed the tip of her cigarette at her husband. "He can judge! He doesn't see her, or talk to her. And then he comes in like he'll fix everything. Pah!" She spat and leaned back in her chair, shrouding her anger in an exhalation of smoke.

"Let me tell you something, my boy," Ray murmured, examining his bandaged side. "Let me tell you something about women. They whine about independence and freedom. And when you give it to them and it all falls to hell—of course it does!—all of a sudden it's your fault. You're this, you're that. And then they want you to pick up the pieces for them! It never fails, I tell you! I don't know how many times—" his voice rose now "—we talk about this. No more money until she respect us! And then I come home," he bellowed, "and I find she trying it again! So I go to try and calm the girl down, you see. I try to talk some sense, just to put a little scare in her. Nothing rough. And you know what that little hussy does?"

Jonah just looked at him. He felt like he was swimming in sewage.

"She stab me!" Ray paused to let the outrageousness of it register. "And while I'm on the bed bleeding, she's out the door and off running. Can you believe that?" he looked at Jonah, expecting him to agree.

Jonah was silent, looking at the floor.

"Her own father," Ray persisted. "She almost kill me."

"Did she?" Jonah asked.

"Ah!" Charlene exclaimed. "Just a scratch on his ribs. He's such a baby!"

"I tell you, I'm sick of it!" Ray shouted.

"Well, what do you want me to do about it?" Charlene muttered. "Nothing I do is good enough for you!"

"Call that sister of yours," Ray replied. "She wants to take Isabella off our hands. She can have her now!"

Charlene said nothing.

"Call her!" Ray repeated.

Charlene looked at him with a poisonous expression. "I won't," she hissed. "I won't go to her with my hat in my hands. I'm sorry, my dear Marie-Therese," her voice became a parody, "you and your high and mighty morals were right—I'm just not fit to be a mother! Here, have my daughter. Have her baptized by a priest, make her into another self-righteous fool..."

"I don't care," Ray shot back. "Maybe she can teach the girl some morals for a change. Call her, Charlene!"

"No!"

Ray leaned forward. "Then I will."

"Do that and you can kiss me goodbye too!" Charlene flicked the burning stub of her cigarette at him. He dodged and it hit the back of his chair, adding another burn mark before dropping out of sight.

"So this is what you want?" he cried, spreading his arms. "More of this until she's eighteen? And you think she's gone then? I bet you anything you want she goes and gets herself pregnant and then we have to take care of her and some layabout's little bastard. For the rest of our lives? No," he shook his head and looked at Jonah. "We deserve our rest, Jonah. It's our turn now!"

"I can't go to her." Charlene's voice was weaker now, crumbling. "My hat in my hands to Her Highness."

"You don't need to, I tell you," Ray said. "I call, I explain everything. Just a while until she straightens up."

Charlene was silent.

Jonah stood, feeling nauseous. "I suppose I should go then," he said. "I have some... studying."

"I'm sorry to bring you out," Charlene peered up at him through her smoke. "Here," she fumbled around on the cluttered table until she found a few crumpled notes and offered them to him.

"No, it's fine," Jonah said. "When we've had a lesson I'll take it."

Charlene sighed. "Well, I don't know about these lessons anymore," she threw a poisonous glance at Ray.

"Really, it's fine," Jonah said. "Just let me know when it's a good day."

Ray snorted. "Good day! I don't remember the last good day!"

Jonah shrugged.

"We call you," Charlene said, almost friendly. "Thank you, Jonah."

"Oui," Ray muttered, stroking his bandaged side. "Thanks, my boy."

Jonah stumbled down the steps and half-ran away. The dog growled from under the house and, when Jonah was a little further away, ventured a bark. But the fight was gone out of him, and he made no attempt to follow. As the Morgan property vanished behind the impenetrable tangle of forest, the nausea in Jonah's gut faded.

He could not count how many times he had arrived to give Isabella her lesson only to find she had run away. On other occasions, he had found her curled up on the floor by her bed, her tangle of blond hair unwashed. She had not even spoken to him then. And when he managed to coax her upright and tried to get her to start a worksheet, she responded with sarcasm and monosyllables. He had spent many of their sessions finding out what was wrong. Sometimes Jonah thought that helped. Isabella had spoken about how much she hated her parents, especially her father.

"He's a pig," she said, staring ahead while she chewed on her nails.

These conversations made her temporarily amenable to a lesson, but she soon lapsed into sullenness, which degenerated into tears and tantrums when her mother tried to make her cooperate.

And there was his attempt to tell her about Mysterion. She said, "My dad says only fools and weaklings believe in anything other than what's in front of them." Facing her implacable derision, he had given up, overwhelmed by the sense of his own inadequacy.

Several yards before he reached the sea road, he turned right onto a barely visible path in the undergrowth and followed it back toward the mountain. He was skirting the edge of the Morgan property, though the house never became visible among the trees. As the path climbed, it vanished, sinking into pools, stagnant and mosquito-infested. Jonah stepped over them without hesitation. He knew exactly where he was going—he and Isabella had taken this path more than once, during the many extended breaks between his attempts at teaching.

She revealed this place to him one day during an unusual bout of friendliness. When he would have continued along the path toward the boutiques where she would buy cigarettes—her usual habit during the breaks—she jerked her head and turned to follow this path. He asked her where they were going, and she smiled with a joy that shocked him.

"A secret place," she said. "Where I talk to the dead."

Vague and fitful before, the path now vanished. Jonah did not hesitate, recognizing the markers from the previous times—the heart-shaped rock on the right, the bent-old-man jackfruit tree to the left. The bushes coated him with cobwebs as they parted to let him pass. Ahead, the graveyard lay as if frozen in its own time. Morning sunlight streamed down through the trees. At the far edge, still sunk in shadows, was the place where she had often taken him.

Isabella sat there now, her knees pulled up into the fetal position Jonah knew so well, while her sleeping face, cold and set and pale, seemed a mere extrusion of the gravestone at her back.

Chapter Twenty-Three

She could no longer feel or see her limbs. They had dissolved into the stream of Okean around her. Light of this brilliance would have blinded her natural eyes, but she could somehow take it all in. Her mind and vision were everywhere and nowhere at once. Her thoughts were perfectly empty, still at last.

After a time—she could not tell how long—the streams of light around her began to shiver, like waves feeling the shore. Before she could articulate the thought, she was into breaking light, then through.

Now the stream of Okean carried her across an empty ocean. She was still transparent, so that everything—water, air, light—passed through her without resistance. The ocean was green, tossed into great waves and teeming with dragons, strange skeletal fish, and immense creatures with flippers. Clouds piled and crowded overhead, shot through in moments by white sunbeams.

As she rushed through curtains of rain and hurricane winds, the clouds vanished, and the water turned from green to the dark blue she knew so well. Blue sky opened above her, broken occasionally as thunderheads burst with storms before dissolving as quickly as they had gathered. The sun rose behind her and set before her in endless succession, flashing like a strobe light in her face. Ahead, the horizon was empty, but even as she flew toward it, a thousand million sunsets flickered, and peaks of land rose above the water's surface.

Swelling as she approached, the islands took on the familiar shape of her homeland. Trees sprouted before her eyes and shot upward, growing over the surface of the land like an instant green skin. Waves of birds flocked back and forth overhead. On the shore, lizard-like shapes lay motionless.

A ship appeared, bucking in the waves just beyond the reef—a blue-painted dhow with a great white sail. An instant later, the dhow vanished, and three ships rounded the headland—square-rigged ships, frigates. They too vanished, and Bella passed the reef and stepped onto the shore. She slowed to glide up the beach, drifting through scenes painted on the air—a couple sat and watched the ocean; a small boy built a sandcastle; shadowy figures danced by firelight.

The sun set and night came.

As she floated up through the trees toward the sea road, couples embraced like ghosts in the shadows; two men furtively dug a hole amid the trees, one holding up a smoky lantern.

The sun rose. Light flooded down.

She followed the road now—a wide beaten path where black slaves in chains and loincloths shuffled up to the plantations; mule-drawn carts groaned under their loads of cinnamon bark and coconuts; ladies, cool-looking in the heat, strolled with umbrellas and muslin veils over their faces; plantation owners in linen suits smoked pipes in the shade; a priest in a white cassock strode by.

Sunset and sunrise, sunset and sunrise. Days passed, more than she could count.

Bella approached her parents' driveway, but it was overgrown with grass and bushes. Perhaps it didn't yet exist. The flickering scenes had changed—the descendants of the slaves now wore tattered clothes and walked with fishing nets or hefted hoes and picks. A well-dressed white couple in an ancient automobile rattled past on the road that was paved now, and the path to her home opened in the vegetation even as she reached it.

A couple strolled ahead of her, entwined together. Bella thought there was something familiar about them, but she was not certain until they stopped in front of her to kiss. Her mother was young and beautiful, and her father's face possessed a gentleness she had never seen. The image overwhelmed her, and then she passed through them like a curtain and they were gone.

She was turning off the path now, along the trail that was freshly beaten at first, but aged and became overgrown with vegetation even as she followed it. The growth posed no obstacle for her, however. She drifted through and up, finding her way, driven forward by the same stream that had carried her before—Okean, now flowing beneath the surface of this world.

Time slowed. The sun floated down. The moon rose like a white spotlight seeking her through the trees.

The heart-shaped rock, the bent-old-man tree, the moonlit grave-yard. Her other self sat against the stone on the far side. A man in a suit squatted with his back to her. Bella drifted among the overgrown headstones, but neither her other self nor Malach disguised as the man in the suit noticed.

The moon descended behind her. From the east, light grew and spread like feathers over the dome of the sky.

Before her eyes, Malach revealed himself, swelling into an immense horned creature. He was holding out the pendant to her other self. The Djinn's lips were moving, and as she passed through him, she wanted to reach and rip his tongue out. But her other self was already reaching out for the pendant as the sunlight pierced the trees and touched the dewy grass. Bella Couteau met Isabella Morgan, just as she grabbed the stone that hung from the claws of the Djinn.

Lethes IV

Isabella Morgan opened her eyes.

Shafts of sunlight dropped through the trees. In the tangle of grass and bushes, the graveyard headstones shone white and tired. Isabella's eyes rested on them. She felt as if she were waiting to sink down into the earth, to lose herself forever in that silence, slowly overgrown and forgotten, while the headstone at her back would keep watch over her until the end of time.

Somewhere above her hung the visions of her life before this moment—the great falls at the Edge of Mysterion, the island of the Elder and the forest of Seeing Pools where she had failed to kill Jonah. Beyond that, the mermaids spoke into her thoughts. At the edge of his one-palm-tree island, the Blind Watchman still floated face down, but she would face that death no more, because now Bella Couteau was running away through the dark trails of Hodoul's island with armfuls of stolen Claw. At night, she slept under the mangrove tree at the edge of the parlay square or wandered like a stray cat through the broken-down shacks. And when the loneliness bit too hard, she climbed through Disagree's windows and curled up on the mattress he had set out for just that purpose. And further still, at the far edge of her mind, stood that hidden island swathed in smoke and fire and the Tree where she had been cast only moments after grasping Malach's pendant—moments so long ago.

And yet it was just a moment ago... Yes, she thought. *It happened just now...*

As if a tide had turned inside her, the memories of Mysterion began to ebb, first becoming blurred, then distant, like an image flowing backward in time. She reached out to grasp at them, but they rushed away from her in silence, growing more distant even as the scene before her—gravestones lit by morning sunlight and almost overgrown by vegetation—hardened, until at last it was the impervious surface of reality, the moment spread before her.

The trees at the far side of the clearing rustled, and Jonah emerged. She recognized him at once but did not wave or call out. He stared at her and started across the cemetery, picking his way around the headstones, occasionally tripping on one concealed in the grass. He got tangled in the out-flung branches of a thorn bush. Then he was beside her, squatting.

Neither of them spoke. In the top of a tree, a go-away bird began to sing. The heat of the day strengthened, turning the air to the consistency of warm oil. The gravestone faces glowed under the sun.

"I thought I'd find you here," Jonah said.

"Did you tell my parents?"

Jonah looked at her. "Of course not."

Isabella shrugged. "I don't know."

"Well," Jonah said. "You should. By now."

"Did they call the police?"

"No. They were talking about calling your aunt though."

Isabella made a face. "Sending me to her, you mean?"

Jonah rocked his head. "They were talking about it."

"They wouldn't have the guts."

"Well." Jonah shrugged. "It's one way out. Better than this all the time."

"All right," Isabella said. "You can stop laying it on."

She stood and dusted off her pants. "I need a smoke. You want to come with me?"

Jonah looked tired, but nodded. "Okay."

For a moment, Isabella looked down at the headstone. She had read it countless times, but now, something stirred as she glanced at the familiar words—a shape of someone she had known, which had faded with the dream of that place whose name she could no longer quite recall.

"Did you ever have the feeling," she said, "that you were someone else, watching yourself do things?"

Jonah eyes were compassionate. "You mean—as if you were inside someone else's head."

"Yes," she nodded emphatically. "Exactly."

"Yes," Jonah said. "I did."

"What did you do?"

He could just detect the pleading in her voice. "One day I woke up and found it was all a dream."

Isabella was silent. At last, she said, "Let's go."

They picked their way across the cemetery, Jonah walking ahead of her.

"One thing," he said as they went. "Before we get your smokes, can we make a little detour? There's something I want to show you." He spoke as if the words might somehow damage her.

"What is it?" she asked.

Jonah did not look around. His voice was still quiet. "You'll see."

"Mysterious!" Isabella exclaimed.

Jonah flashed a brief smile back at her. "In a way."

Isabella was aware of the trees shrieking with birds, the weight of the sunlight, the silent depths of the earth beneath her. Everything now seemed to conceal something else, everything somewhere else. In that moment, she allowed some great weight to collapse upon her. And instead of being crushed, she found herself buoyed upward in a tide of lightness.

"Yes," she said. "All right." The memory she had glimpsed looking down at the headstone now resurfaced, sharpened into a more definite form—a man with skin like lava from an ancient volcano, a bald head like a beacon, and something else about him... Glancing back at the headstone, she murmured, "His ancestor was a slave."

"What's that?" Jonah said.

"Nothing," she replied. "I just remembered someone. Keep going."

She broke into a jog to catch up with Jonah, as he flashed a smile back at her. Together, they reached the edge of the cemetery and entered the trees, heading back down the hill toward the sea road.

Deserted, the clearing fell once again into the quiet of the dead, a quiet somehow heightened by the racket of birds squabbling for fruit high in the trees. The sun arched overhead, baking the headstones before descending into the tree line where Jonah and Isabella had gone. Just before it did so, however, a few of its rays touched the east side of the clearing and the face of Isabella's favorite headstone. The rays, tinged golden by dust, played on the stone's surface, underscoring the worn and fading etching of the inscription carved in hasty letters:

Jean De Sagré

Did you enjoy this book? You can make a big difference!

Reviews are the most powerful tools that I have when it comes to getting attention to my books. Although I'm not a starving artist, I don't have the financial muscle to take out full page ads in the *New York Times*.

But I do have something more powerful than that.

A committed, excited, and loyal group of readers.

Honest reviews of my book help bring it to the attention of new readers. The more reviews it has, the more Amazon "notices" it. At a certain point of interest, the Amazon algorithm can actually help make my books "more discoverable."

If you've enjoyed my novel, I invite you join my Reader Group by signing up here: http://eepurl.com/cTN5X1

I would also be very grateful if you'd spend only five minutes to leave a short review on the book's Amazon and Goodreads page. You can jump straight to that page by clicking below:

amazon.com/author/www.richardgarciamorgan.com

https://www.goodreads.com/rgarciamorgan

Thank you very much!